Also By Dannika Dark:

THE MAGERI SERIES
Sterling

Twist

Impulse

Gravity

Shine

NOVELLAS
Closer

THE SEVEN SERIES
Seven Years

Six Months

Five Weeks

ACKNOWLEDGMENTS:

This book is dedicated to a character who wouldn't stop
pacing around in my head until I told his story.

The heart is an anchor cast to sea,

That links you *closer* to destiny.

CHAPTER 1

INIQUITY POOLED BENEATH KANE'S FEET in shades of liquid burgundy against the gritty asphalt of the dark alley. The tips of his black boots scraped against the shadowy surface. One of the laces had sprung loose and touched the vile evidence of his evening walk. It was too dark to see the blood soaking into the tight weave of fiber, but when he lifted his foot off the ground, a drop splashed onto his other boot.

Shit. My favorite pair, he thought, dragging his eyes back to the crumpled body beside the brick wall. It wasn't as if he had extra money in his pocket to buy new boots, and now these were toast.

The middle-aged man was slumped over on his left shoulder like one of those crash-test dummies after an accident.

It was against Breed law to kill a human.

The murder was so fresh that a bead of sweat still trickled across the man's balding head like a slow-moving insect. His right leg and arm were extended, giving him the appearance of trying to run. Only this worthless splinter of a man was going *nowhere* except straight to hell where he belonged.

Kane glanced down at the pain and rage still dripping from his fingers in red liquid light and mingling with his own guilt.

Emotions are always richest in the end and the hardest to wipe clean. Death holds on to the threads, sinks into the crevices, and becomes an impossible emotional experience to erase.

Kane was a Sensor in the paranormal world. No unique physical characteristics made him stand out from anyone else on the street. His lifespan was longer than a human's, but what made him genetically different was that Sensors experienced the world through touch—something Kane avoided like the plague.

Last winter, he'd settled down in Cognito after years of traveling. Kane had lived in twelve states and must have had several dozen jobs since he'd left his troubled home as a teen, only to become trouble himself. It had taken a few years to shake some of that wildness out of him.

Cognito was home to more immortals and other Breeds than anywhere else in the United States. The Breed were bound by laws to keep the supernatural world hidden and social order maintained. While he kept to himself most of the time, being around his own kind didn't make him feel like as much of an outsider. It wasn't that he didn't like humans; Kane just felt like an impostor around them.

During his travels, he'd discovered just how many different Breeds existed. The first time he'd met a Mage was in a New York City train station when he was looking for a place to stay. Unlike in popular fiction, they didn't work magic but rather harness energy in the most unimaginable way. Then there were Vampires, and from his experience, most of them were jackasses. They had powerful dark eyes that could pull the truth out of anyone.

Most of the Shifters he met were decent and left him alone, except for the wolf packs. They were difficult to get along with because they were territorial. Sensors had a lot in common with Shifters because both could have children and grow old. *Eventually.* Not all Breeds aged the same.

Kane was in his thirties, but he looked much younger. He still had all the etchings of an older man in the tiny lines around his eyes and the shadowy grooves of his cheekbones. It was great to dip into the fountain of youth and not age as quickly as all the humans around him. He made sure to keep his spirit as youthful as his looks. He watched his favorite bands at the local dive, played pool, and had no desire to become the bitter old man his father was.

Kane's gift as a Sensor allowed him to lift emotions effortlessly. Objects retained traces of any intense experience, making Sensors ideal for investigative work. But the real money was in memory exchange. A man could sell his memory of a sexual experience to a Sensor, who would store that emotion and then offer it to the highest bidder. Customers would attest that a quality Sensor made the experience better than the real thing.

Sensors place their hands on the donor's chest for the best reception. Energy then flows through their palms, creating a ruby-red glow. Sensors were an exchange service, and those with heightened abilities made some serious cash. Advertising was by word of mouth or through samplers—usually candy spiked with emotions to give people a taste of their wares. The Breed looked at Sensors as a form of entertainment.

He'd tried it once when he was desperate for cash. Went into a Breed bar and discovered it wasn't easy to collect emotional imprints unless you had something to offer. So he stole an experience from a drunken man sitting against the restroom wall and barely conscious. Once Kane got the guy talking, he placed his hands on the man's chest and recounted a memory of a motorcycle chase. It was a painful experience because Kane was hypersensitive to emotions and felt them to the extreme. But he was hungry and needed a place to stay.

Kane had walked to another bar—uncertain of how to go about it—and asked around. With only one memory in his collection, there were no takers. Finally, one guy offered him enough to pay for a decent meal and a bed for the night.

"This better be worth it," the Shifter had said.

Kane nervously touched the guy's chest and released the memory. Unfortunately, physical contact caused him to feel the experience all over again—something he hadn't anticipated since it was his first time dealing. Kane grimaced as a smile spread across the Shifter's face and a look of exhilaration filled his eyes.

Never again.

Not long after that, Kane had run into a guy in a tattoo parlor who hooked him up with work as a deliveryman. It was a Breed company run by a couple of Shifters, and it was the kind of job where he didn't have to interact with people outside of a random signature or two. Lifting boxes also saved him the expense of paying for a gym membership since the heavy shipments toned up his arms. It wasn't the best-paying job, but it had its pros and cons. It was enough to swing rent, and that was all that mattered.

Kane had realized in his twenties that he was different from other Sensors. They'd developed a way to desensitize themselves to touch—like turning down the volume—but Kane found it impossible to shut off. Even the light brush of a hand triggered an avalanche of emotions that felt more like a violation of his senses.

That was why he always wore gloves. *Almost* always.

His fists clenched in an attempt to expunge the emotions still tethered to his bare skin from the kill. Had he worn gloves while committing the crime, they would have been as good as a confession if they fell into the hands of another Sensor. Plus, they were his favorite pair, and he didn't want them muddied up with this unplanned incident. He'd never killed a man before.

Kane hadn't left the house that night with the intention to commit murder. He had strolled out of the corner market with his dinner in a paper sack and made a detour to the newspaper stand. His pocket jingled as he fished out a few coins. Kane glanced up as a pretty blonde dashed across the intersection. When she slipped into the back of a taxicab, her skirt blew up. He grinned, always enjoying the moments when people assumed no one was watching. That was when a man bumped into Kane and made him spill his change.

"*Shit*. Watch where you're going," Kane barked out, expecting an apology.

One of the quarters bounced into the street and rolled into the drain. Kane pressed his lips together tightly and glared at the man. He liked reading the comics late at night in bed while eating a bowl of cereal and wearing nothing but his grey sweatpants. It was one of the perks of being single. Not to mention that he needed to look at the classifieds and find a new place. His landlord had refused to fix the air-conditioning and then raised the rent on his lease, which was why he was now having a difficult time making ends meet.

The bald man lifted his pointy chin and gave him the finger

before disappearing into a narrow corridor. Kane set his bags down, ready to give the little shit a piece of his mind.

"Hey, where do you think you're running off to?" Kane said, grabbing the man's upper arm. "You owe me a quarter."

They were in the middle of a dark alley, and a dog barked in the distance. Kane sized him up, realizing this guy might want to start a fight even though he didn't look like the type. He was stocky in build but shorter than Kane. Beady eyes glared up, and then the human wrapped his hand around Kane's bare wrist. With a quick motion, the stranger pulled himself free and walked away.

That one touch set a chain of events in motion.

Kane's hazel eyes glazed over, and he saw a wake of bodies in his mind. He was standing face-to-face with a serial killer. Death wasn't just a stain on this human's hands; it was a bold tattoo. So many young women—so much pain.

Men like that didn't deserve to breathe the same air as the rest of them.

Kane was faced with a choice: let a murderer who would victimize even more women walk the streets, or do something about it. The memories of violence assaulted his senses again, and he stood on the brink of a decision that would alter more than one life. There was no evidence he could use to bring this man to justice in the human courts, and yet these crimes would weigh on his conscience if he didn't do something.

Now.

He stripped off his gloves and tossed them on the ground, making a comment that stopped the human cold in his tracks. "*I know what you did to those girls.*"

The man slowly peered over his shoulder, and his eyes widened. When he started to run, a dark side of Kane surfaced and exploded into action. He reached for the switchblade in his back pocket—one he'd only ever used to slice apples.

"Come back here," Kane growled, quiet rage funneling through his soul.

Something compelled him to take action—maybe it was the voices of the victims crying out for justice. Without a second to think, Kane reached out and sliced the man's jugular in a single motion with the sharp blade. Blood poured from the mortal's neck, and he stumbled to the ground, taking only moments to die.

Kane was numb.

What have I done? He wiped the flat edge of the bloody switchblade against his black T-shirt and stared at the body.

Breed had insiders within law enforcement who investigated crimes, concealing evidence and bodies that linked back to one of their own. Most of them didn't like humans, but cutting one up in a dark alley wasn't going to win him any awards. Didn't matter if the little shit deserved it. Now Kane was going to have to leave the city he'd grown to love. He'd heard stories about Breed jail, and it scared the hell out of him. No one ever came out of that place the same as when they went in.

Cognito was a far stretch from his childhood home, not to mention the fact that he'd been raised by humans. Kane hadn't known he was different until second grade when his dad shook him for tipping over a glass of Kool-Aid onto the white sofa. His father had shaken him so hard it fractured his arm, and he'd peed in his Superman pajamas. Kane had been so distraught that his own father was hurting him that, through his tears, he tattled on his dad for having sex in the back seat of the family van with a woman Kane didn't know. It had just flown out of his mouth, and his mother stood in shock. At that age, a kid didn't know what sex was, but on the way home from school, he'd felt the dirty emotions mixed with guilt in the back of the van. He often wondered if he'd never spilled that drink if his relationship with his father wouldn't have fractured like his arm.

Hell, maybe the man had never liked him. Kane could sure feel his disdain whenever he touched him, which wasn't often.

When his younger sister came along, the arguments between his parents got worse. There was so much sadness and anger in the house that Kane had gradually stopped touching people and often wore long-sleeved shirts. He didn't have sex until his twenties—a late bloomer—and by then, the gloves were his thing.

In the dark confines of the back alley, he analyzed the crime scene, trying to put himself in a detective's shoes. Traces of the act lingered beneath his feet, but it wasn't as if his name was written on the wall.

Kane flicked his eyes up, expecting his name to appear on the brick building in front of him along with a large arrow pointing down. Vampires could pick up information in the blood, but they never drank from a dead body. Worst-case scenario? If they hired a Chitah. Not spelled like the animal, but they shared the same predatory traits. Those quick bastards could track his ass down, and Kane was on foot tonight. Chitahs had an acute sense of smell, were unbelievably fast, and they never gave up on a hunt.

He messed up his brown hair with his fingers, thinking about the groceries left by the newspaper stand. His night shouldn't have ended like this.

Some lucky son of a bitch is going to feast on frozen lasagna and a six-pack while I'm running for my life, he thought.

Bile rose in his throat when he glanced down at a plastic sack with a box of condoms peeking out from the opening. It would be a long time before Kane would be able to shake the imprint of this night off his conscience.

Run? Hours could go by, and a Chitah would still be able to track his scent if he remained on foot. His heart pounded as he glanced around. There wasn't a single friend to call or place for him to hide out. That's what happens when you're a loner; no one is there for you when you need a friend you can trust.

"Shit," he muttered, tugging at his left earlobe. It was a nervous tic of his whenever something upset him. He got a piercing when he was seventeen and was always messing with it until he eventually took it out. Since then, tugging at his ear had become a habit.

A set of car keys glittered in the broken moonlight beside the dead man's feet. Kane jogged over to where he'd dropped his gloves and dusted them off, stretching his fingers inside the breathable fabric. He felt naked without them. Kane nervously scrubbed his fingers through his hair again, which he kept in disheveled chunks on top. It was razor cut, giving a rebellious look to his charismatic features. Once he got his shit together, he strolled over to the body and bent over, lifting the keys with a flick of his wrist.

"On second thought," he muttered, squatting down and staring at the body. Kane fished inside the man's pocket and swiped his wallet. Stealing the car might buy him some time, but not much if the cops discovered who this psycho was and tracked down the license plates.

"Fuck you, John Doe," he said, giving a two-fingered salute. "I hope all your victims get their revenge on the other side."

Kane sprinted in the direction the man had been walking and wound up in the center of an old parking lot. There were only five cars, and he ruled out the newer models because the keys were designed differently than the one pinched between his thumb and index finger. When it wouldn't fit in the green pickup truck, he walked twenty paces to a white four-door sedan with tinted windows. It reminded him of those car-chase movies he used to watch on Saturday nights after work. The key turned, and the lock clicked open.

After a quick look over his shoulder, he got into the car and shut the door. It smelled like musty cigars, and Kane wrinkled his nose. There was a magazine rolled up between the maroon seats and a can of soda in the cup holder.

Now what? he thought, rubbing at his bristly jaw.

Kane flicked his eyes up to a shadow that was moving around a few yards ahead. He leaned over the steering wheel for a better look. A mangy old dog sniffed a strip of fabric waving in the breeze on a chain-link fence. Kane leaned back and chuckled as the mutt lifted his leg over a pile of crates and took a piss. The dog sniffed in circles and found a rolled-up paper bag by the fence. After a few attempts, he managed to get his teeth into it and trotted off with his prize.

A car backfired in the distance, and Kane adjusted the rearview mirror, staring at himself. Not many men had hazel eyes as captivating as his. They were a beautiful olive green on the outside with a splatter of orange in the center, as if an ink pen had leaked from his pupils. His brows arched into a wicked slant that gave him a look of mischief.

Kane pulled off his right glove and wiped his sweaty palm down his jeans before adjusting his seat. The adrenaline wasn't wearing off, and his heart was galloping out of control. If he

didn't take some deep breaths and chill, he was going to pass
out.

"What the fuck are you doing?" he muttered.

The wallet creaked as he folded the leather back and
memorized Mr. Psycho's address. Instead of getting his ass
pulled over in a stolen car while looking for a junkyard at two
in the morning, it made more sense to drive to the owner's
house. He could dump the car and go on foot from there.

"Andrew Butcher," he said, staring at the license of a
smiling man with a gap between his teeth. "Are you kidding
me? A. Butcher?" He gave an exasperated sigh and tossed the
wallet in the passenger seat. Andrew was the kind of guy who
might have squeaked by as a normal citizen, but something evil
lurked behind the steely eyes in the photo, which made Kane
uneasy.

The ignition turned over with a noisy complaint, and the
engine sputtered, coughed, and decided to start up.

Kane's black boot punched the gas, and he wondered if it
was a good idea to leave the scene so quickly. Had he left any
evidence left behind? The last place he wanted to end up was
in Breed jail, because punishment never came with parole or
a second hearing. You served your time if proven guilty, and
the accommodations were not stellar. A guy at work had spent
fifty years in one of their small cells and didn't have a favorable
thing to say about it. A death sentence would be an act of

kindness in comparison, and if you received one of those, it was carried out within the month.

He drove for over an hour, trying to locate the address by using a map he'd found in the glove compartment.

The fan belt screeched as he slowed down on a long, shadowy street. It wasn't a picturesque neighborhood, either. The dilapidated houses looked fifty years old, and even the twisted roots of the trees looked like they were trying to escape. Two dim lamps cast eerie silhouettes, and most of the houses had iron doors that resembled prison bars. Creepy would have been a compliment.

"Twenty-eight, twenty-nine… bingo."

The siding on Butcher's house looked as if it were made from roof shingles, and the evergreen bushes in front of the windows were out of control. Kane leaned against the steering wheel and stared at a garage big enough to fit one car, evidently with an automatic door since it lacked a handle. The keychain didn't have a clicker, so he ran his hand along the top of the visor until he found a small clip and hit the button to open the garage.

As the car rolled up the driveway, he flipped the headlights off and took one last look around. Once the car was inside, he pulled out the key, and the engine hissed like a poisonous viper. Kane got out and scoped the garage for a second clicker to shut the door.

"Shit. Where did you hide it?" he whispered, pacing around the dark room that smelled of paint fumes.

Maybe Andrew Butcher had only one. If so, when Kane decided to leave, he was going to have to lean inside the car, hit the button, and make a dash beneath the garage door before it shut on him.

His worn boots tapped against the smooth concrete behind the car. As he scanned the neighborhood one last time, his bare finger slid along the edge of the trunk.

Kane froze.

It felt as though a fingernail had ripped away from his skin and exposed the quick. Alarm raced up his spine, and his heart pounded against his chest. A repulsive combination of terror and exuberance licked at his fingertips from the residual emotions left behind. Kane doubled over, stomach heaving as he struggled not to throw up all over his shoes.

A body was inside the trunk.

CHAPTER 2

KANE HAD ALWAYS BEEN HYPERSENSITIVE when it came to his abilities, but he had allowed his own fear and adrenaline to cloud the human's emotions, which he should have picked up on with his ungloved hand.

The imprint on the trunk door was strong, but there was no fear or pain, which meant that Butcher had killed his victim before the body was put into the trunk. That evil little prick had enjoyed every minute of it, too.

Kane turned the key, and the trunk lid popped open. The hinge creaked as it rose up, and all he could make out was a shadow of... a woman?

A draft blew in from the open garage, reminding him that he was about to unveil a body in front of the whole fucking neighborhood. Kane reached for the clicker on the passenger seat and waited for the door to close. Once he had privacy, he flipped on the light switch by the door to the house.

"What the hell am I doing?" he said under his breath through clenched teeth.

"Locking myself in a maniac's garage with a dead body, that's what," he answered. "Probably has a wife and kids inside, and I'm about to expose the truth about what Daddy has been up to."

He quietly turned the knob to the house and peered inside to see a small kitchen with a brown linoleum floor. In fact, it looked like the color brown had thrown an orgy in there and smoked a cigarette when it was finished. Brown cabinets, walls, countertops—even the shutters. He quickly noticed there were no flowers, cookie jars, oven mitts, or other decorations. It lacked a feminine touch, and that brought a sigh of relief. Just a sink full of dirty dishes and a white garbage bag stuffed in the corner by a pantry door. Not to mention a giant bottle of bleach and three rolls of duct tape.

He shuddered.

The house was small and thankfully empty. Kane wedged through a broken door in the short hallway and stood inside the dingy bathroom. The reflection staring back at him could have been someone else. Is this what a murderer looks like? Tiny spatters of dried blood peppered his right arm. Kane flipped on the hot water and scrubbed himself clean.

Another wave of nausea churned in his stomach from all the things he was handling, and he felt the human's intent from earlier that evening. It wasn't nearly as strong as touching a person, but cookie-crumb emotions were always left behind.

A patchy scruff on his square jaw showed how lazy he'd been that morning when he decided to skip shaving and sleep in. Still, it suited him. Kane's mouth curved up a little on one side, giving him the appearance of smirking about something wicked. But the ladies never seemed to mind kissing him. His nose was straight and centered, drawing attention to his hazel eyes. They were the magnet that always made an undecided woman change her mind. He was a good-looking guy, but Kane never liked to be noticed for his looks.

His reflection didn't seem to have any sage advice as it gave him a scolding appraisal.

A thought flitted through his mind, and suddenly Kane couldn't breathe.

What if she wasn't dead?

He spurted out profanities while running down the hall. Kane damn near killed himself when he stumbled over a flimsy red rug in the living room. It didn't have rubber lining on the bottom, and he slid, losing his balance until a telephone table broke his fall. He flung the door to the garage open and walked toward the car to look inside the trunk.

A swath of brown hair covered her face, and the first thing that captured his attention was her light blue dress. It was the style all the girls were wearing that summer in Cognito—delicate and strapless.

He'd never touched a dead body before, and his stomach twisted into a tight knot. What would he feel? He slowly brushed the hair away from her face with his gloved hand. The sight disgusted him. Blood smeared down her cheek and pooled on the floorboard beneath her head. When his eyes slid over to the tire iron lying at her feet, Kane suddenly wanted to kill the son of a bitch all over again.

A rivulet of blood snaked across her nose, and Kane reached down with his bare hand to feel for a pulse.

For a split second, a brilliant light blinded him. When he opened his eyes, he unexpectedly found himself standing in a spacious, unfamiliar room. Sunlight poured through the windows like water from a pitcher, but not the morning sun. It was a beautiful shade of afternoon gold. A snowy white floor gleamed below his feet, and the dim walls hovered like a thick blanket of fog.

It was so startling that it took several seconds before he noticed the transparent image of a woman before him, the one whose slender neck his outstretched arm was touching.

"Who are *you*?" she asked in a voice edged with fear.

Kane snapped his eyes open and hit the back of his head on the trunk lid as he stood up.

"What the hell was that?"

He clutched his chest, staring down at her fragile body. Nothing like that had *ever* happened to him before. Ignoring his throbbing head, Kane leaned against the garage door and cursed.

She was *alive*.

It wasn't the faint tick of a heartbeat against his fingertips telling him that, but the flicker of life that reached out to him through their link. That touch was dull in flavor, but it left a taste on his palate that incited his curiosity. There was an absence of background noise—no emotional turmoil of past deeds, anxiety, or other feelings that consumed people.

Kane could touch without feeling.

There was also something else. She wasn't human; she was *Breed*. The emotional energy of a supernatural and a human was different, like comparing decadent chocolate to a peanut.

God, what had that bastard done to her? The hem of her dress had a piece torn off, and she wasn't wearing any shoes. Long brown hair covered her shoulders and spread across her bloodstained dress. Strands of it stuck to her face, and the roots were a rich shade of mahogany at the site of her injury.

Still alive.

Kane paced in the confined space of the garage, heart racing in his chest. He retrieved his black glove from inside the car and slowly stretched his fingers into it, giving himself a minute to think. What was he going to do with her?

Had she been a human, he could have dropped her off at the emergency room, but Breed didn't allow one of their own to be kept by human prisons or hospitals. Too risky.

Maybe a Relic could help. Knowledge was passed down genetically through their ancestors, which gave them unique information about different Breeds. That was their gift, and most became consultants or healers of some kind. Kane didn't know any Relics, let alone someone who wouldn't turn him in to the authorities in a heartbeat for his crime.

He tugged at his left earlobe and leaned against the dirty car. The thought of leaving her entered his mind and quickly evaporated. Kane wasn't that kind of guy. Taking her to his house was out of the question because parking a stolen car outside while he carried an unconscious body upstairs would only guarantee him a stupidity badge. And then what would he do with her?

"*Shit, shit, shit*," he muttered, kicking his heel against the tire.

Kane walked around the car and raised the trunk lid. It took him a minute to get a firm hold on her, and then he lifted her gingerly into his arms. The strange thought entered his mind that he'd never carried a woman before. Guess he'd never been the kind of guy who swept a girl off her feet.

He was gentle, and when her head rolled against his chest, he gripped her a little tighter. His biceps firmed into hard muscle as he carried her through the house. Kane shouldered the door open to a small guest room and placed her slender body on the dark green bedspread, careful not to jostle her wounded head.

"Hey," he said, lightly shaking her shoulder. "Can you hear me?" With the tip of his gloved fingers, he wiped a few clumps of hair away from her face. "Rise and shine."

When her left cheek touched the pillow, he got a better look at the gash on the right side of her head and grimaced. The hall light was bright enough that he could see she was still bleeding.

Kane kicked in the broken door to the bathroom and rummaged through the cabinets for clean rags and towels. He ran three of them under scalding-hot water before returning to the room to sit beside her. It took a little effort, but he managed to clean up the mess from the misery of her night, revealing quite a lovely girl beneath.

She had such feminine cheekbones and soft features that he couldn't help but stare. Her lashes were three shades darker than the light brown hair that fanned across her chest. A speck on her left cheek stole his attention, and he brushed the little flat mark with his gloved thumb, but it didn't rub away. It was a beauty mark.

She was the kind of woman that guys like him admired from the other side of the glass. Some days he stood on the curb, discreetly peering over his shoulder at the women inside the gourmet candy store, escorted by doting boyfriends with fat wallets. He especially loved that shop because of the orgasmic looks on their faces when they were in the presence of expensive chocolates.

"I'll get you all fixed up," he promised.

Her matted hair was stubborn to clean. Kane did the best he could, wiping away the caked blood surrounding the deep gash just under her hairline. Despite the revelation that she wasn't human, he couldn't tell what her Breed was.

Curiosity got the better of him, and Kane pried her left eyelid open. Sometimes you could tell what Breed a person was by the color of his eyes.

A crooked smile slanted up his cheek. "Brown," he murmured.

Kane had always liked brown-eyed girls. He thought there was something so warm and beautiful about that color, and hers were a pale brown, reminding him of the New Mexico plateaus at sunset—earthy, warm, and rich with mystery.

Had he imagined being in that room with her? If so, then it was time for a big dose of therapy and a bottle of happy pills. But if not... *if not*, then she was in there somewhere trying to reach out. Probably scared as hell. The link between them didn't seem possible; a Sensor never had visual manifestations during a connection.

He bit the tip of his finger and pulled the glove off his right hand; the cool air felt sweet against his warm palm. With a gentle press, Kane laid his bare hand on her shoulder and closed his eyes.

"Get out of my head!"

She swung out her arm and struck him with a metal object.

"What the f—" He snapped open his eyes in the bedroom and bent over, clutching his head. "That fucking *hurt*."

A small knot throbbed beneath his fingertips, and when he glanced over his shoulder at the empty room, he realized how insane this was. Somehow, this girl had managed to injure him through pure thought.

How was it possible?

He narrowed his eyes, angered by her lovely mouth and the ungrateful tone that had flown out of it.

"Don't do that again, do you hear me?" he warned, leaning in close. "I'm… ah, shit. I'm talking to an unconscious person. Look, if you're in there and you can hear me, then I just want to see…"

See what? If she was offended by a stranger hopping inside her head and touching her?

"Jesus," he muttered, rubbing his jaw.

Kane decided to give it another shot. He placed the flat of his hand across her collarbone and closed his eyes.

Suddenly, he was face-to-face with the woman, his arm outstretched. She wore a scowl like a fashion statement and swung a large frying pan in her right hand, struggling to push him away.

He blocked the hit with his left arm, and it made a clang as his knuckles struck the hard metal.

"Ow! Shit, that *hurts*!" he growled. "Stop it. I'm trying to help you."

"Help me?" she said patronizingly. "Why don't you start by taking your hands off me? Because it looks more like you're helping yourself."

He tried. Damn if his hand wasn't glued to her chest. When he pulled his arm back, she stumbled forward and gasped.

"I can't. It won't come off," he said with confusion.

She stepped away from him with fear in her eyes, but all it did was force Kane to follow her. The pan swung out again and this time he caught her wrist.

"Stop hitting me with that damn thing! This is—" He flicked his eyes all around. "You're unconscious. I'm a Sensor, and I can tell you're also Breed."

Her eyes softened a little, and that stubborn jaw went lax.

"That's right. There's a link between us, and whenever I touch you with my hands, I wind up in here."

Her brown eyes sharpened, and she kneed him in the groin. Pain sliced through the lower half of his body, and he dropped to his knees.

"Then come back when your hand isn't three inches away from my breast!"

Kane's eyes flew open, and he fell backward, hitting his shoulder against the hard floor. He stayed that way for about ten minutes, with one leg still draped over the fallen chair, while he allowed the ache in his balls to subside. A moth flitted about and settled on the popcorn ceiling.

There was quietness in their connection, and he realized that he couldn't feel her anger, unless you counted the pulsing pain in his head and groin. He lifted his left hand and peeled back his glove far enough to see that his knuckles were beginning to bruise. That link allowed him to feel all the physical stimulation her mind inflicted upon him without having to deal with the emotional bullshit.

To touch without emotion. His cheeks flushed thinking about it.

He kicked the chair over and sat up when something caught his eye. The bloody lace on his boot was an unwelcome reminder of why he was there in the first place, so he untied his boots and kicked them off.

Kane sat beside her and pushed his index finger between her eyes.

When the flash subsided, he was back in the room in front of the woman, pointing at her forehead.

"Try again," she said sharply, and slapped him hard on his left cheek.

His face stung like a bitch when he opened his eyes in the dark bedroom.

"Goddammit!" he shouted at the unconscious woman. "You know, you're a pain in the ass," he chided, waving a finger at her. Kane angrily got up and stood in the open doorway. "I have a mind to just walk out and leave your ass," he said, but didn't really mean it.

Kane didn't work that way. He had a soft spot for women,

even though he kept dating to a minimum. He was the kind of guy who stepped in if he saw another man talking down to a woman. It didn't matter if they were married; he made sure she was okay before giving that jerk a piece of his mind. But relationships? Not really for him.

It was too complicated to find someone who accepted his firm commitment to wearing gloves in the bedroom.

Energy transmits through the hands, yet it was muted when someone other than a Sensor touched him—another reason Kane dated outside his Breed. Intense emotions always leak, so Kane became a master in the bedroom at turning women in positions where they couldn't touch him.

Kane had had a fling with his boss's sister until one evening she decided to take casual sex to relationship status. She came from a family of panthers, and that scared the shit out of him. The last thing he needed was to piss off her family with a bad breakup and be torn to shreds in a dark alley by a group of merciless Shifters. Although, she *was* a good sport about the gloves, not to mention a wildcat in bed.

Literally. The second she stripped down naked and decided it was time for him to meet her animal, Kane was the *hell* out of there. Didn't even put on his jeans when he caught sight of her shifting.

The bed bounced when he finally sat down beside the girl and held her left hand. Kane drifted back to the mysterious room. Pale golden light sifted through a small window. He sensed the walls more than he could see them, and near the window was a small wooden chair.

"Better," she said in a calmer voice. "But I don't make it a habit to hold hands with a stranger without knowing his name."

He tilted his head to one side. "I'm Kane."

"Is that your real name?"

He slanted a brow at her tone. "Yeah, why? What's wrong with it?"

"Just sounds like an important name, and you don't look very—"

"Well, it's my name," he ground out.

Her soft brown eyes lifted up to meet his gaze. She showed poise, standing tall with a confident lift of her chin, even though Kane was a few inches taller. He'd never met a woman with such an expressive face, whose mind he could read just from a subtle quirk of her mouth. The palest of pinks colored the apples of her cheeks. It was a relief to see the blue dress without bloodstains, and it had a soft swish to the ends. Yet it was the shoes he noticed most of all. They were white sandals against vibrant blue nail polish. It stood out because she had been barefoot when he'd found her.

"Why are you here, Kane?"

"Do you know where here is?"

Her hip jutted out to one side, and it was comical to watch

her attitude surface despite the fact that they were holding hands like a couple of lovebirds.

"It's *my* head; I should know what it looks like."

Kane looked around. "Lady, you sure have an empty head."

She narrowed her eyes. "Oh, I'd love to see what's in *yours*. Empty beer cans and adult magazines?"

"I don't read porn," he growled.

She smirked triumphantly. "So you're not denying the beer."

Few women had the ability to ruffle his feathers, and yet she more than ruffled them—she plucked them out one at a time.

Her eyes lowered to the ends of his tattered jeans. "Why did you take off your shoes? It's too cold in here to be wandering around in a pair of socks."

"Can you wake up?" he asked.

She suddenly jerked her arm back, and Kane lurched forward, losing his balance. He almost grabbed her dress and tore it off as he fell to his knees.

Women shouldn't have such short tempers, he thought.

"I have a whole arsenal of imagination on hand," she threatened. "Don't get any ideas, because I can make this unpleasant for you. If I could wake up, I would have already done it, don't you think?"

Kane dragged his eyes up the length of her body. He took his time doing it too. Long, silky legs disappeared beneath her thin dress, and he imagined himself wrapping his hands around her narrow waist. The fact that she wasn't wearing a bra beneath her dress didn't escape his attention; it was enough to titillate the male mind. He'd never seen such beautiful skin—it just glowed.

When their eyes met, she sucked in a sharp breath and her cheeks turned a deep shade of pink. Man, if *that* wasn't enough to make him shift uncomfortably on his knees. Kane got that look a lot. A lover had once told him he had smoldering eyes— the kind that could undress a woman thread by thread until she was blushing and naked. Only now, Kane was the one who felt like blushing. She intimidated him with the way her body immediately responded when he looked at her.

"What's your name?" he asked her in a voice that was hoarser than it should have been.

She didn't respond. Her tawny brown hair tumbled forward and framed her cunning face. Kane had never felt so exposed by a woman's gaze.

"Well, if you won't tell me your name, then why do I smell cookies? Are you really so bored in here that you're baking?"

A change blossomed in her expression, and all the anger withered away, replaced by an emotion he couldn't read. "You can smell that?" she breathed.

He nodded, remaining on the floor. She seemed less intimidated by him when he was in a submissive position, and he wasn't in the mood to fight off another frying-pan attack.

Kane involuntarily smacked his lips, not realizing that the

fragrance of sweets had awakened his hunger. He swallowed hard when he noticed that her eyes were fixed on his mouth.

"Do you have any family that I can call?"

She slowly shook her head, appearing fragile—like one of those little glass ballerinas on display in the gift shops. "How do you know about the cookies?"

Enough of this shit.

Kane shot up to his feet and glared down his nose. "Peanut butter cookies, to be exact. Give me the phone number of a relative, and I'll call them to come get you. Maybe they know a Relic or someone more qualified than me to pick your convoluted brain."

A baseball bat appeared in her right hand, and she tapped it against the white marble floor. "I was thinking about my grandma," she murmured. "But no one has ever…"

Kane jerked her hand to snap her out of whatever fog she was in. "Friends?"

"No, we're *not*," she replied sharply, brown eyes narrowing to slivers as she looked defiantly up at him.

"What I mean is do you *have* any? I'm guessing by the way you give introductions with a fucking cast-iron skillet that the answer is no. If you raise that bat, I'm not going to play nice."

Her voice raised a pitch. "Well, if your definition of *playing nice* is feeling up a helpless woman—"

"Helpless?" He snorted. "Lady, you're about as helpless as a rabid porcupine."

That's the last thing Kane remembered.

CHAPTER 3

W HEN HE AWOKE ON THE floor beside the bed, it was with one hell of a sore face. Yet it was the blow to his ego that hurt more than his eye. He'd been in his fair share of fights, but had never once gone down for the count. That woman could have been a prizefighter.

After working the kink out of his neck, Kane got up and went into the living room. It didn't appear that Mr. Butcher had entertained visitors very often, judging by the deplorable condition of his house. The plastic cup on the coffee table had black mold floating on top of whatever liquid it contained, which was no longer identifiable. He sat on the squeaky sofa and leaned forward, glaring at the porno magazine beneath a dirty plate with dried ketchup smears. The page that was dog-eared had a woman strapped to a bed with tape over her mouth. Kane turned his eyes away and twisted a clump of hair between his fingers.

Maybe the best thing to do was to just leave her and call the cops. Kane tightened his lips and shook his head. If they found out she wasn't human, they'd turn her over to a bunch of scientists to play with.

"Shit."

Abandoning her was out of the question. He wouldn't be responsible for putting her in the hands of some wannabe dreaming of a Nobel Prize at the expense of a woman's life.

Kane absently tugged at his earlobe and looked around. The walls had a yellowish tint—probably from the cigar smoke. In front of the small television was one of those green swivel chairs that looked like a garage-sale purchase. A huge stack of DVD cases filled a bookshelf next to the television. He remembered the duct tape on the kitchen counter and didn't want to imagine what was on those videos.

Kane's gloved finger traced along a rip in the knee of his jeans, and he shivered when the air conditioner kicked on. Everything about the house was frigid, like an empty grave.

He muttered a curse while rubbing his sore jaw. Stealing the car had been a royally stupid idea, and now he was trapped inside a serial killer's house. He couldn't call a cab because the last of his money was sitting inside a paper bag by the newspaper stand.

The fabric of his thick socks stretched when he wiggled his toes. Kane suddenly remembered the comment she'd made about it being cold in there. He sprang up and crossed the room to a thermostat mounted on the wall beside a faded photograph of an old woman. Duct tape held the box together. When he slid the lever five degrees warmer, the air immediately shut off. He wandered into the bedroom with the hall light shining in from behind.

Dirt covered the soles of her feet. The thought of what that sadistic animal had done to her burned like a hot coal in his stomach. Why would any man inflict that kind of cruelty on a woman for his own pleasure? It disgusted him, especially knowing that most Breed were far more protective of women than humans seemed to be.

He flexed his ungloved hand and draped a thin blanket over her slender legs. How could someone so feminine have so much fight in her? He'd never seen such an angelic face—she glowed, and he thought about how radiant she must have looked in the sunlight.

The bleeding had finally stopped—a good sign. Head wounds could be messy, even if they weren't very deep. Kane knew this because after a night of drinking when he was twenty, he'd wound up on the receiving end of a wine bottle held by one pissed-off Mage. The bartender had thrown them both out, and Kane had ended up on the list—the one that all Breed places keep of people who break the rules about fighting on the premises. Some turned a blind eye if they were paid enough, but most of them didn't give a shit who you were.

He focused back on the girl. Stitches were definitely in her future.

An idea crossed his mind. He sat beside her on the bed and stripped away his left glove.

"Let's see you take a swing at me this time," he said with a smirk. Kane held *both* of her hands—nice and tight.

When his eyes snapped open, one belligerent woman was turning her mouth to the side. It wrinkled up her lips in the most amusing way, and he flashed a devilish grin at her as she tried to free her hands.

"No more hitting," he said in a serious voice. "What's your name?" Kane noticed in his peripheral vision that she was slowly tapping the toe of her shoe against the floor. His lip twitched.

"Pocahontas."

"Well, in that case, it looks like I've captured me a squaw."

"How's your face?" she asked, shifting her hip in a way that caught his eye.

Kane sniffed out a laugh. "As handsome as ever."

She rolled her eyes and blew a strand of hair away from her face.

"Let's sit down," he suggested, already moving to sit Indian style and pulling her down with him. It was too awkward to stand there like a couple of school kids holding hands. This way, they were at eye level, not to mention that he wouldn't have to dodge her temperamental knee.

She reluctantly followed his lead, sitting on her left leg. "Why didn't I just die?"

His breath caught unexpectedly at the vulnerable bend in her voice. Her brown eyes turned solemnly to the floor, and Kane immediately regretted the harsh words he'd said to her. This was just a girl who'd gotten herself mixed up with the wrong guy—her anger and fear were understandable.

"What's your Breed?" he asked in a thick voice.

"Sensor."

He almost broke the link. "You don't transmit like a Sensor; I'm not picking up anything."

"That's because I'm defective," she said, averting her eyes.

Clearly it was a sensitive topic, but he'd heard of such things before. Some of them were dead receptors, unable to collect emotions. Some could transmit, but with only a vague awareness of the quality, so there were a lot of pissed-off buyers. Intolerance was an unfortunate reality among Breed when it came to imperfections.

Kane relaxed his grip and lowered his voice. "Defective in what way?"

Her fingers flexed, but it only tightened their grip. "Meaning I'm a dead transmitter—a one-way channel." Her jaw punched out, as if daring Kane to make fun of her. She didn't appear to be ashamed of it, just used to the intolerance. "I can pick up emotions all I want, but there's no point. No one can feel *me*," she said, stressing the last word.

That was a big deal, too. Kane knew the disdain she must have faced in the bedroom when the men discovered the sex wasn't going to meet their standards. It was something he strongly related to since most Sensors didn't give him the time of day when they found out that he wouldn't share. Sex was another little perk when it came to their gifts, because they would exchange the experience during the act. You could feel each other's pleasure, and it intensified the rush.

He sighed, compelled to tell his own story. "I'm… I don't know how to explain this." Kane was about to spring something personal on a woman he'd just met—something he didn't talk about with others. "I can't handle touching anyone. I pick up way too much shit and can't shut myself off from drowning in it."

"That's the first thing you learn to do as a child," she said in disbelief.

His voice became abrasive at her remark, and he started putting up his wall again. "Well, no one ever taught me. I've heard about Sensors being able to disconnect from the emotions—"

"Not disconnect," she said, correcting him. "It's learning how to desensitize yourself so you don't become overwhelmed. It's kind of like a numbing agent during the exchange. Why didn't your parents show you how to do it?"

"Are you going to tell me your name, or do I get the honor

of making one up for you? Because I have a few words in mind if you want to hear them."

Her luminous eyes nailed him to the ground. "It's Caroline. But I don't go by that; everyone calls me Carrie."

A lump formed in his throat, and desire consumed his body like a raging inferno. How could a name elicit such an intense reaction? The kind that made his heart stammer in his chest to the point where he coughed to make sure it was still beating. The unanticipated attraction he suddenly felt for her startled him. The softness of her small hands linking them together and the intensity of her gaze filled his chest with warmth.

Kane lifted his eyes, and his anger crumbled away. "Caroline," he whispered. "That's pretty."

She turned her head to the side and parted her lips, touching her chin to her bare shoulder. Passion filled Caroline's face— the kind he only saw on a woman when he buried himself deep inside her and she came undone.

Then again, maybe he was just misreading her.

How do you politely tell someone to get the hell out of your head? Carrie was having a difficult enough time dealing with her situation, let alone having to contend with a stranger forcing his way inside her mind.

Kane hadn't been deterred when she lashed out at him

more than once; he kept coming back for more. She was still shaken from the assault, and his unexpected appearance put a fright into her.

But it wasn't until he said her name that the anger dissipated. His tone was so intimate that she'd had to look away. There was a craving in his voice that made her feverish, a thickness in his timbre that covered her arms with goose bumps.

No one called her Caroline, and certainly not the way he did.

Earlier that evening, Carrie had been watering the ferns on her patio, watching the nine-year-old next door blowing bubbles onto the street from her balcony. The couple that lived there fought constantly, so Carrie would leave small gifts inside the empty flowerpot for Jesse, their little girl. It was a short reach through the bars with only a foot between balconies.

The sidewalk chalk had been a mistake. When the mother saw a garden of beautiful flowers drawn on the concrete, she'd made her daughter scrub them away. After that, Carrie left simple things like bubbles and freshly baked cookies, and only when the babysitter was in the living room blaring her heavy metal music. Jesse never spoke, but she would smile sometimes and peek at Carrie through the railing. She was a shy little thing.

There was just enough light in the sky to make it to the diner and back home before it became too dark to walk the streets alone. One of those flame-broiled hamburgers with fries sounded fantastic. The guy behind the counter had a crush on her and usually threw in a free vanilla milkshake with three fresh cherries. He knew that it would keep her there a little longer, because Carrie would sit at the counter and eat them before she headed out. He was nice, but a little young for her taste. Still, she loved how his eyes would light up when she walked through the door, and maybe that was one reason that she stopped in once a week and flirted with him through small talk.

He had never had asked her out; maybe he was too shy. Carrie always liked a take-charge guy, so it was probably for the best. She was a softy when it came to the romance movies— not the ones in modern times where they meet in a bar and a tumultuous relationship ensues, but the ones with knights and men of honor. However, the bigger issue with the guy at the diner had nothing to do with his personality. He was a human, and that was a big no-no.

Carrie had dated a few Sensors, but once they found out about her defect, they left nothing but skid marks. Most of the men approached marriage like an arrangement, selecting a woman with the best skills. Where's the romance when they're appraising you like a car on the showroom floor? And her engine wasn't a six cylinder, but only a four. No one wanted a disabled child, so men were selective when choosing a partner. Then there was the whole sex thing. Sensors all but demanded transference in the bedroom—it heightened the experience like nothing else. She could receive just fine, but they couldn't.

That was *always* the deal breaker.

On the way home from the diner, Carrie crossed the dimly lit street, sipping on her vanilla shake. A stray dog's toenails clicked on the sidewalk behind her, and alarm ran up her spine. He might have just been hungry for the burger in her sack, but it wasn't easy to distinguish Shifters when they were in animal form. Wolves and dogs were particularly troublesome because they ran in packs. In any case, it wasn't on her agenda to get rabies, so she cut through an alley, hoping to shave off some time.

The deliciously cold milkshake numbed her lips, and she curled the warm paper bag against her chest, staring at the chain-link fence that blocked her inside the vacant parking lot.

"Lovely," she muttered, turning on her heel. A pebble rolled inside her sandal, and she tapped her toe on the broken concrete to shake it out. The sun had already set, and she was anxious to get home before her favorite show came on.

Carrie cautiously glanced around and blew out a breath when she noticed the dog was nowhere in sight. As she headed back toward the alley, a white sedan crept around the corner from a back entrance on her left. She was alone and felt acutely aware of the slow speed of the car. Her heart thumped nervously against her chest when a bald man cranked the tinted window down. He was stocky and sweating profusely.

"Need a ride?"

She dumbly shook her head, the paper sack growing heavy in her arms. The engine shut off, and he opened the door to get out. The car blocked the exit, and her eyes darted around the empty lot. Carrie was breathing faster, feeling the adrenaline pour into her veins.

As he stepped around the car and approached her, Carrie sensed malice. His emotions were blazing like a forest fire. Dark intent dripped from him like honey, and the second her milkshake splashed on the concrete, Carrie was on the run.

Dry, dusty air burned her lungs. *Not fast enough*, she thought, hearing him closing in behind her. She kicked up pebbles with every step. There was no chance of outrunning this man in her sandals, so she leapt on the fence to jump over it.

He gripped her ankle, pulling off her shoe as she desperately kicked him until he let go. Carrie lost momentum and twisted over the fence; her dress snagged and ripped at the end as she fell on the hard ground. An open field of wild daisies and tall weeds stood between her and a row of buildings on the far side. The fence rattled as the man began scaling it, and that's when she took off again. Halfway across the field, a sharp rock pinched her heel, and she fell down hard on her elbow.

Before Carrie could move, a knee rammed into her lower back, and a strong hand brutally shoved her face into the dirt.

"Think you can get away?" he said mockingly. "Nope. Nobody gets away from me, you little tease."

"Please, don't," she tried to say. But the press of his knee cut off her breath, and she cried out.

This couldn't be happening. *Someone* had to see what he was doing. Her eyes pleadingly skimmed up to the buildings, searching for a face in the dark windows as pain lanced up her side.

His strong arm hooked around her waist, and he covered her mouth with his callused hand as they stood up. That was the moment when she realized he wasn't going to assault her in that open field. He was *taking* her, and that's when she knew she was going to die.

Not like this. Not like this, she thought.

Carrie bit into his hand and clawed at his arms like a feral animal.

"Goddammit!" he growled in her ear, shaking her like a rag doll.

Fear iced through her veins. Carrie could only breathe through her nose, and she was panting so hard that not enough air could get in. Her heart pounded with such intensity that it felt like it was going to explode. The attacker had no hair to pull, so she reached back and scratched his face with her short nails. That's when he threw her on the ground and kicked her hard in the stomach. She curled up, gasping for breath.

The heart-shaped ring she always wore was lying in the dirt, and Carrie slipped it back on her finger before he noticed.

It was just a trinket, but one that she never took off because the ring had been a gift from her father.

Dirt muddied her tears as the flavor of his intentions leaked from his pores.

She tried screaming, but it came out ragged and pained— her stomach tightened and she wanted to throw up. He was mumbling to himself when he picked Carrie up and dragged her through the gate. Her other shoe fell off as her feet left long trails in the dirt.

Her eyes went wide when she saw the open trunk of his car, and Carrie sank her teeth into his arm, deep enough to draw blood. She stumbled when he let go, and without warning, he backhanded her. Carrie hit the ground behind the bumper and looked over her right shoulder, too numb to feel the scrapes on her arms and legs. That's when he lifted the tire iron from the trunk.

As he raised his arm, a single word trembled on her lips, barely anything but a cry through the sobbing that left a trail of tears down her dirty cheeks.

"*Daddy*."

Years had passed since she'd seen her father, but Carrie needed him to hold her in that final moment and tell her that everything was going to be okay. *Please God, I don't want to die.*

The first swing landed on her back. The second one she couldn't remember.

The memory lingered as fresh as a raw wound while she gazed through the empty window. She was a prisoner in her own mind, which was probably for the best. God knows what that man was doing to her body, so maybe it was a blessing that she remained unconscious.

When Kane had first appeared, it startled her because he wasn't a figment of her memory or imagination. A striking set of hazel eyes and furrowed brows stared past her as his fingers touched her neck.

It scared her that someone could get inside the safest place—the only place—she had left. Not to mention he had his hands on her. The second time he returned, she had a surprise waiting for him. Kane might not have meant her any harm, but how could she have known that when every time he appeared, he was touching her?

"*Caroline*," he whispered. "That's pretty."

While sitting on the cold floor holding hands with a stranger, Carrie distinctly felt Kane's beautiful eyes drinking her in. He wasn't the sort of guy that ever gave a girl like her a second glance either. Hearing her full name roll off his tongue brought a heat to her cheeks; it was intimate, and she liked the idea of someone calling her by a name that no one else used. When the blush faded, Carrie met his riveting gaze head-on.

She hesitated. "What did he do to me?" The thought of being raped crossed her mind and terrorized her even more than the beating. "Was I… Did he…"

"No," he said in a firm voice. His dark brows slanted sharply. "It looked like he was just getting started when I found you in the trunk."

"Good," she said on a trembling exhale. "The last thing that I can remember is him trying to get me into the car. Then he hit me with that metal thing." She instinctively winced.

Kane lifted his arm and tried to touch his ear before dropping their hands on his lap. "I took care of him. Look, we both know that I can't take you to a human hospital. Give me a number of someone to call. Maybe a Relic could help, but I don't know any. Do you?"

She shook her head. Carrie's father had once consulted a Relic when she was a little girl and they found out about her problem, but the Relic had merely stated there was nothing he could do. *It happens.*

Kane seemed keenly interested in their hands. Between their short conversations, he would look down and slightly turn them, as if contact was something that he wasn't used to. What an odd reaction from a Sensor. Maybe he didn't like the fact that he couldn't feel anything from her. She was insecure about her defect, not because it mattered much to her, but because it did to everyone else. Enough that it altered her chances of having a family and children. Carrie loved life, but there were sacrifices that she had learned to accept.

Her mind drifted back to her grandma's kitchen, a place where she'd always felt at home because Grandma was the only mother Carrie had ever known. She clung to the memories in order to stay grounded, because part of her was feeling adrift.

A strong aroma of peanut butter and chocolate-chip cookies filled the air, and Kane's nose twitched again. His tongue slid out, running along his lower lip and lingering at the corner. She squeezed his hands without even realizing it, and he smirked.

Kane was savagely handsome. He was the sort of man with smoldering bedroom eyes that her coworkers would have called *smoking hot*. Not a guy who needed to approach women, because his aloofness and wolfish grin was all the bait he needed. Whenever he bent his arm a little, his toned bicep would flex, and she stole glimpses when he wasn't paying attention.

Carrie had never dated a man so nicely built and sexual as Kane. Her dates were usually smart, well-dressed guys with boring office jobs. They were the kind of men who were in search of a wife, not a lover.

Compared to his warm tan, Carrie felt like an Irish albino. He encased her small hands with his large ones, and his skin was so deliciously hot. Kane's thin, black T-shirt was a snug fit, and his jeans were tattered with a few rips. The fact that she was physically attracted to the man kindled her irritation.

"Exactly how is it that you're able to get inside my head? Mind explaining that, Mr. Houdini?"

"Only if you explain how these battle wounds are showing up on my real body," he said, lifting his bruised knuckles.

Was he serious? That was impossible.

"You're only saying that to make me feel guilty. I just had a man try to murder me, so forgive me if I'm not rolling out the welcome mat."

A red carpet rolled across the floor, and she blinked it away in embarrassment.

His eye *did* look swollen, and a quick glance at his knuckles revealed a small cut. How was it possible? He could smell her grandmother's cookies, and that was only something she was thinking about. Kane's connection was so unique that fear and excitement shared a little dance before going their separate ways.

"Kane, I want you to wake me up."

He chewed on his lip for a second before answering. "Give me a number."

"There is none." She made a frustrated sound. "I don't have any family."

Carrie was an only child, raised by her father. He'd disappeared when she was fifteen, and after that, life had been temporary housing with other kids her age until she was old enough to find work. That's how Sensors ran things. They had a small Council, but they only stepped in when it was their duty. Carrie enjoyed the freedom of living alone even though she'd spent a few sleepless nights wondering what had happened to her father. *Had he abandoned her, or was he involved in something illegal?* The most difficult questions in life are always the ones without an answer.

"I'm sure you've got somebody—a boyfriend?"

"My friends are just a couple of people at the hotel where I work as a desk clerk. That's what happens to girls like me who aren't like the other Sensors—not that I would have wanted to get into trading. They're just casual friends, and we don't even talk outside work; I doubt they'd want to be tangled up in whatever's going on here. Exactly what *is* going on here? Who are you?"

"I'm nobody," he replied, attempting to pull his hand away. "I'm just a guy who was on my way home when I ran into your friend."

"He's *not* my friend," she bit out angrily. Another thought crossed her mind, and her heart skipped a beat. "What if he finds out where I live?"

"You don't have to worry," he assured her. "I took care of him."

She swallowed hard. "Took care of… how?"

The sharp line of his jaw intimidated her when he clenched his teeth. "Meaning he's dead. I don't think he had time to do anything to you, because he was in a hurry to get back to his car."

"Why were you going through his trunk? Where are we now? I don't mean here," she said, looking around. "Where are we for real?"

His teeth scraped against his lower lip. "His house."

Carrie paled.

"What?" she cried out, catapulting to her feet. The guilt on his face made her furious. "You mean to say that you found me unconscious in the trunk of a car and decided that instead of calling for help, you'd drive me to that murderer's house? And then—then you appear in my head with your hand on my chest! If my hands were free, I'd slap the living shit out of you! How dare you—"

"Now cut that out!" he roared, standing up so that he towered over her. "It's not like that. I didn't know you were in the fucking car. The plan was to dump it at his house and wash my hands of this catastrophe. Going to Breed jail to rot for the next century is not on my agenda, you got it? I could have left you right where you were, but that's the sort of thing a lowlife would do. I'm not saying that makes me a hero, but cut me some slack for trying to lend you a hand." He smirked inwardly; the remark could have been funny considering they were holding hands. "If you don't want to help yourself, then I don't know what else I can do."

"Don't *want* to?" she said in a broken voice. "What choice do I have? What can I give you that'll wake me up? I don't have anyone." She fought against angry tears. "I'm stuck here and fading to God knows where, and you want to blame me for not being able to get myself out of this mess. Well, I'm *sorry*!"

Too late. Wracked with emotion, Carrie completely lost it

and fell to her knees. All she had wanted was a milkshake and a compliment. She cried against her arm, thinking how silly it was to wonder if the guy at the burger place would notice when she stopped coming in. She had been thinking off and on about getting a puppy to keep her company in her quiet apartment.

All the things she had never done—all that life wasted. How was she to know that this could be the last night of her life?

Hot, salty tears streamed down her face, and the man with the hazel eyes knelt before her and tenderly squeezed her hands.

"Go, just go," Carrie choked out, barely audible. Now she had to cry in front of this man because she couldn't let go of him, and that made it so much worse.

"Hey, hey now… don't cry," he said in a soft voice. "You're going to be okay, Caroline. Do you understand me? I'll figure something out."

He wiped her wet cheek with the back of his knuckles, and it didn't seem to matter that he was still holding her hands. Kane had a firm grip and a soft touch, as if all his emotions were in every stroke, and yet she felt none of him in this place. Within the walls of her mind, the only pain she felt was her own.

"I'm sorry I hit you in the head with a frying pan." She sniffed, finally gaining the courage to look him in the eyes once more.

Kane snorted and sat back. "I've been told I have a thick head. Don't sweat it." His Adam's apple undulated when he spoke in a gentler voice. "What did you mean when you said you were fading?"

Fear snaked in her belly, and she furrowed her brow. "Did you notice how the light in the window seems to be a little bit dimmer?" she asked, nodding in that direction. "What if that means something?"

Kane looked thoughtfully over his shoulder at the stream of light that blanketed the room like a golden tapestry. "Just means that you need a lamp," he said, trying to sound like it didn't matter.

She wiggled her fingers and noticed that his hands were clammy. Funny that you really didn't need to be a Sensor to know how someone felt if you just took the time to read their body language. It was in the way he tightened his jaw and briefly avoided eye contact that showed he acknowledged what was happening. Did he care? Probably not. Maybe he just didn't want to deal with anything this heavy, and who could blame him?

"I think that's my light," she said. "It feels like I'm separating from life, and the scariest part is there's no feeling of angels or someone waiting at the end of a tunnel. Maybe that doesn't come until later, but I'm not ready to die. I'm really scared, Kane."

"Don't sweat it," he said with a lowered brow. "Look, you

just need to sleep it off and heal naturally. It'll take a while, but you'll get there. It's not like we're human—we don't die as easily."

That was true. They were mortal, all right, but all Breed had the ability to heal slightly faster. Sensors, like most Breed, were also resistant to human diseases. They lived longer than Relics, who were the closest to humans genetically and had a shorter lifespan, not to mention that Relics were more susceptible to catching airborne viruses like the flu. A Sensor who took care of himself could live a couple of hundred years, sometimes longer.

A serious take-charge look came over him, and a bloom of confidence invigorated Carrie when he leaned forward. Sometimes all a person needed was a dash of hope to get through the darkness.

He squeezed her hands. "Caroline, did you hear me at all when I wasn't in this room with you?"

She almost didn't hear the rest of the sentence after he said her name. Carrie would have liked to hear him say her name over and over again. In fact, she purposely delayed answering him.

"Caroline?"

She quirked a knowing smile and quickly concealed it. "I'm not sure. Maybe—but I wasn't paying attention."

"Here's what I'll do: I'm going to leave for a few minutes to see if I can wake you up. Concentrate as hard as you can. Got it? Listen for my voice and try to follow it. Maybe somehow I can pull you out of here if we keep trying. Your head injury just looks like it needs stitches, but I don't know—if he hit you with that tire iron…"

Kane twisted his mouth skeptically. He didn't have to say another word. A few stitches? She might have a cracked skull and brain damage.

Carrie nodded, and in the blink of an eye, Kane was gone.

CHAPTER 4

"CAROLINE, TIME TO OPEN YOUR eyes," he said in a commanding tone. "Can you hear me? Follow my voice and come out of there."

Kane put on his gloves and shook her gently at first, but then with more urgency. He was careful not to jostle her head because he hadn't inspected her injuries as thoroughly as he should have.

She didn't respond. He'd never expected to have a decision so completely placed in his hands, where his actions meant life or death. Especially not in the same night he'd committed a murder. Maybe this was karma giving him a cosmic bitch slap. Kane stood up, tugging at his earlobe.

The bright green numbers on the alarm clock switched over to the next minute. Exhaustion wouldn't rub away. God, what if he fell off the bed and cracked his skull during one of their head hops? Kane snorted. Wouldn't that just be ironic?

Sirens wailed in the distance. He walked to the window

and peered through the curtains at the sleeping world. When the sounds faded, he recognized them as fire trucks and not police sirens. Tell *that* to his thundering heart.

Kane crawled onto the bed on the other side of Caroline and propped his head in his hand. The idea of lying beside a woman was kind of nice; something he did only on rare occasions. She had such soft lines to her body, curves in all the right places, and a lovely skin tone. He looked between their arms and noticed how much richer his tan was. Her face was angelic, not carved with the hollow cheeks and sharp lines of a tough woman. The expression she carried was serene—absent of worry, pain, and anger.

"Caroline?" he whispered softly.

Kane's stomach knotted when he glimpsed the dark bloodstains on her blue dress. It offended him, because now he knew how lovely it looked on her—the way the fabric swished when she moved around. It also conjured images of what that son of a bitch had done to her. He thought about removing her dress, but then what? He sure wasn't going to put that bastard's clothes on her.

Her eyelids fluttered, and he leaned in closer.

"Wake up," he said firmly.

Kane considered for a moment where to touch her. The handholding was awkward—a gesture he never indulged in and wasn't sure how he felt about it.

After all, it wasn't his hand that most women wanted to hold.

When Caroline had begun to weep and the tears splashed on his hands, it was all he could do not to bolt out of there. He preferred it when she was spitting hateful things at him because it was less personal. The idea of soaking in her sadness with their hands still joined frightened Kane.

But to his surprise, he felt nothing in her touch.

Fear morphed into relief and then wrapped back around to fear again. Why didn't he pick up anything with her? She wasn't able to transmit, but Kane had always been a highly receptive Sensor.

"Damn," he hissed, lightly touching the sore lump on his head.

Kane grinned, thinking she was a ballsy little thing and he liked that. She might not have been able to escape her attacker, but he knew that she'd given him a hell of a fight. Caroline possessed tenacity and spirit—there was nothing dull about her.

After a good rub of his tired eyes, he cursed himself for lying in bed next to a coma victim and deciding she was date-worthy. Not to mention the fact that she had kicked his ass and showed zero interest in him. It wasn't a big surprise; Kane never talked to girls like her because they always ended up with a doctor or Councilman. She was out of his league, and it had nothing to do with whether or not she came from money. Some girls were just like that. It was the smooth way they spoke, the intelligence behind their bright eyes, and the sophisticated way in which they moved.

Kane removed his right glove and placed it on the blanket between them. A small silver ring with a turquoise heart captured his interest. It was on the pinky finger of her right hand and looked like something a child might wear. He hadn't noticed it before, but suddenly Kane was curious about the little things. Had someone given it to her? Was there a special meaning?

He slipped her delicate fingers into his right hand.

"What took you so long?" Her eyes were rimmed with dark terror.

He didn't like that look, and it worried him enough to circle his gaze around the room and pull her closer to him.

"What's wrong?"

"Why did you leave me here for so long? You said it was only going to be for a minute or two."

The light was noticeably dimmer.

"How long do you think I was gone?"

Her bare shoulders lifted, and she shivered. "Seemed like hours."

But it had only been minutes. "Did you hear me calling your name? Think carefully. Did you sense it in any way—or maybe something around here changed?"

A lock of her silky hair slipped in front of her nose, and he fought back the urge to tuck it behind her ear.

"Maybe a whisper, but I thought it was the wind. It's getting colder in here, Kane. I'm not dressed for… for death."

She attempted to laugh, and he smiled, giving her credit for keeping a sense of humor given the circumstances. But the comment was a spear in his conscience. *This won't happen*, he thought. *I won't let it.*

When she shivered again, he guided her to the window and they sat down against the wall, underneath a spray of golden light. Caroline sat on his left, and he leaned in her direction with his knee bent. His right hand held hers as if they were shaking hands. Strange. Kane was getting used to touching her, and he shifted his body so that she would be comfortable.

"Better? The sun will warm you up."

But that didn't seem to put her at ease, and he noticed the ghostly expression on her face. Caroline kept her eyes low, but she was watching him out of the corner of her eye.

"Kane?" She scarcely breathed.

"Yeah?"

"What if you smothered me with a pillow?"

Chills rolled down his arms, and he swallowed thickly. "What?" he bit out. Kane's intense eyes were the epitome of a blazing inferno. "You think I would do something like that? Is that the kind of man you think that I am? Why would you even—?"

She cut him off and swallowed him up with those glittering brown eyes. "You know that feeling in the pit of your stomach before you get on a roller coaster? The line is long and everyone is waiting their turn. You hear the screams and convince yourself that it's no big deal—until you see the green faces of the people getting off, like maybe it wasn't such a good idea. I'm in that line, Kane. Except I'm not able to get out or cut ahead. All I can do is wait my turn. That roller coaster is roaring in my head, and I'm scared."

Caroline blew out a shaky breath, and Kane tensed when she slid closer. He lifted his arm and draped it around her bare shoulder. She didn't just accept the invitation—Caroline molded herself against him until it felt like they were one. The flat of her left hand slid across his stomach and balled up the black T-shirt, as if he might try to escape.

"You're so warm," she said in a small voice. "There's just not enough of you to wrap myself up in."

Those words incited an unexpected need to protect this woman. He discreetly dipped his nose in her soft brown hair and took a shallow breath. It made him want to go back and stomp on the ruthless bastard who had done this to her. What could he possibly say that would offer her any comfort?

"Hey, what if I tried to transfer some of my emotional energy to heal you?"

"Won't work," she countered. "You know the rules."

"It works with strong emotions," he insisted.

"Yes," she agreed, lifting her stubborn chin. "But the only Sensors who are ever successful at it are loved ones. We can lift, store, and transfer—but it takes something far more powerful to convert it into healing energy. That only comes from love. It won't work if you just sit there and think of your dead puppy or your first breakup."

"Have you tried it? I don't remember seeing that written down in the manual."

"*Here* we go," she interrupted. "Mr. Know-It-All thinks that he's going to part the Red Sea and work miracles like no other Sensor has done before."

"Don't do that," he muttered. "You're the one suggesting that I asphyxiate you with a feather pillow. I'm just offering an alternative to suicide."

"Don't do *that*." Caroline pushed him away, and guilt flushed her face like burgundy roses. Their hands were still joined, but Kane felt a wall go up and divide them.

Fear makes a person contemplate things they wouldn't normally do—he got that. She was entitled to a weak moment, so he backed off. He couldn't imagine having to go through something like this alone, and maybe that's why he wasn't in a rush to leave.

The pretty blue dress draped over her knees like a breath of summer air. She had lovely legs, and he especially liked the faded freckles on her shoulders. Probably something she got as a kid. And why did the image of her in pigtails and punching all the boys appeal to him so much? He smirked inwardly as his thoughts skated away from him.

Caroline was a bit like his spirited little sister—they both were strong-minded women with soft hearts. Sunny was never physically aggressive with anyone, but she could put the hurt on a man with that mouth of hers. Sunny was a different brand of girl and the only family he had, even if they weren't related by blood.

"What are you thinking about?" Caroline wondered aloud. "Your expression just switched off for a minute there. What's on your mind?"

"My sister. I was thinking about my sister."

"Oh," she quietly replied. "What's she like?"

"You remind me of her, except that Sunny doesn't cuss."

Caroline snorted. "Well, jeez. You make me sound like a foulmouthed sailor."

He lightly squeezed her hand. "I've only heard her swear once. That's not to say she doesn't have a rare moment or two; it's just that the words are pretty tame. She probably doesn't remember this story. It happened when she was a little thing, I'd say about three or four years old. Just guessing." He shrugged.

Caroline curled up her legs and pulled the dress over her knees. "What happened?"

Damn, he hated the memory, but it felt good to confess a part of his past that had bothered him for so many years. Most women didn't want to hear stories like this, but Caroline did. Kane rubbed his thick arm and rewound the hands of time.

"Sunny was a pretty baby with blond curls. Spoiled as hell. At least, she was at that age. Not in the way that gets a kid a bunch of toys and junk—our parents were cheap—but they sided with her a lot, and she always got her way. Things changed when we got older. I think my mom thought having Sunny would fix what was wrong in our family. So I was jealous of her since I was the firstborn."

"Naturally," Caroline agreed.

"She didn't talk until she was three, and she picked up this really annoying habit of parroting everything I did or said. It drove me fucking crazy," Kane said with a chuckle. "I was a snot to her. I'd slap my face so that she'd do it to herself and stop copying me. Damn, I hate that I did that," he murmured, suddenly revolted by his memories of indirectly harming his sister.

"You were just a kid," Caroline offered. "She didn't know better, and neither did you."

He sighed, moving on. "Well, I started learning all kinds of new vocabulary."

"Where do boys learn that stuff?" she asked with amusement.

Kane lifted their hands before dropping them onto his lap. "Magazines we shouldn't be reading, older brothers, movies, friends at school—you name it. I taught Sunny to say one of those words and—" Kane thumped his head against the wall punishingly.

"What was the word?"

"We had a cat, and I thought it would be funny to teach her the *other* word for cat." He flicked his eyes nervously at her. "You know—pussy. Anyhow, one night after her bath, I went into the bathroom and saw that no one had drained the tub. The cat wandered in and I tossed it in the water for a laugh. It went wild, almost tearing the shower curtain down as it scrambled to get out of there. I was laughing my ass off when it flew through the house like a bat out of hell. There was a huge trail of water leading to the kitchen, and Mom came out yelling. Sunny walked in right when it happened and she started to cry, thinking that I'd hurt the cat. The next thing I knew, Sunny ran into the living room yelling *Kane got my kitty wet*."

He rubbed his eyes as if he could erase the memory. "Only, it wasn't *kitty* that she said."

"Oh," Caroline said in a quiet breath.

"My dad had a conniption and flew off the sofa. It was one of those split-second moments as a kid when you realize you've crossed a line and you're about to get a spanking. An innocent joke escalated into pandemonium."

"How old were you?"

"Old enough to know better. Ten. I turned around to run into my bedroom and lock the door when I caught sight of him going after Sunny. His anger just exploded, and she was the nearest person to him. When we were kids, Dad was never a violent man to us outside of the usual spankings. He was a drunk who used to berate our mother. It was a vicious cycle, and she never left him. When he grabbed Sunny's arm, I snapped."

Unable to scrape his fingers through his hair, Kane slowly closed his eyes and spoke in a dark voice. "Over my dead body was he going to lay a finger on my sister. The next thing I knew, I was charging through the house like one of those bulls in Spain. Mom went into hysterics, and he swung me against the wall."

"Oh my God," she breathed.

"Then the predictable bastard left the house to get drunk at the bar. Sunny might not have been my real sister, but I saved her from getting the beating of her life."

Kane shook his head, remembering how destroyed he'd felt as a kid when his father had handled him roughly and lost control.

"Sunny didn't know what was going on. Dad's finger had left a small bruise on her arm, so after that, I did right by my sister. I realized that the stupid stuff I'd chosen to teach her could get her into trouble someday. That night changed me. I made sure that Sunny never cussed and that she always had what she needed. We still had our fights like any brother and sister, but I looked out for her. It's been well over twenty years, and the scared look in her blue eyes when I tucked her in that night still haunts me."

A thoughtful moment passed and Kane appreciated the silent reflection.

"Does she live here?"

"No," he replied guiltily. "Last time I saw her was in Texas. That's not where we grew up, but it's where she moved when she left home. We haven't seen each other in over a year; it's probably about time for me to pay her a visit. She's stubborn about taking my money, so I sometimes leave it with her best friend."

"You're a good brother, Kane. Despite what you think, you brought her up right and still look out for her. Not many ten-year-olds have the foresight to see how their actions can indirectly impact the kind of person someone else becomes."

Caroline slid her left hand across his leg, and his muscles locked up. It was instinct, the same way you might flinch before someone slaps you. Except all he felt were her smooth fingers on top of his jeans, gently stroking as if she wasn't aware that she was doing it.

Man, was *he* aware. A lump formed in his throat, and he distracted himself from his thoughts by staring at the highlights in her hair.

"You said she wasn't your real sister. What did you mean by that?" Caroline asked.

Another sore topic.

He inhaled loudly and sighed. "Talking about my past isn't helping your situation," he said, glancing around the empty room. The walls looked like they were made of smog, and it was noticeably dimmer. The light left a warm, satiny gold blanket across the floor, as if the sun was fighting against being snuffed out like a flame.

"Maybe not, but when you talk it calms me down. Please don't stop; I really want to know more about you."

"I've never told anyone this," he began.

She snorted. "Who am I going to tell? Really, Kane. Think of me as your confessional, because you have zero chance of this ever getting out. Was she adopted?"

"No, I was. They were human."

Caroline sat up and gave him a pensive stare. "What?" she almost gasped. "You were raised by humans?"

Might as well have been wolves, he thought to himself. They were genetically different. Kane had neither experienced what his body was truly capable of, nor had he learned how to refine those abilities at an early age. As a result, it became a detriment to him. It was like being born a Thoroughbred and living in a pen with no training until you were mature. No one had taught him how to harness his skills, so he'd been running wildly out of control while the others stayed on course at a steady pace.

"Yeah, my parents were human," he said, trying to avoid her inquisitive eyes.

At some point, Caroline had inched closer to him. Most

women looked at him with desire, but she looked at him in a completely new way that he wasn't comfortable enough to accept. It was invasive and personal.

"What happened to your real parents?"

Kane made a frown that was the equivalent of a shrug. "That's something I'll never have an answer to. I was always different, and my dad figured it out early on. It wasn't until high school when I found out just *how* different I was from everyone else. By then I'd stopped touching people because of a few bad experiences I'd had with a couple of girls I dated."

"Why would that be bad?" she wondered aloud.

He quirked a brow. "I'd never felt sexual desire directly from another person, and it scared the shit out of me. One girl was a little more experienced than I thought, and when I touched her neck during our first kiss, she was definitely thinking about someone else."

"Slut," Caroline muttered.

Kane tried unsuccessfully to contain his smirk.

"Another time, we were planning a garage sale, and everyone was digging through the house to find old junk we didn't need anymore. I went through my mom's cedar chest and found a small blanket. The minute I touched that thing…" Kane pressed his lips tightly together, and Caroline turned his chin to look at her.

"Tell me," she said.

"My abilities amped up. You know how strong death is. It clings."

She nodded, no longer sitting up but lying against his chest with her ear pressed over his anxious heart.

"I accidentally touched a drop of blood on the blanket and experienced the residual pain of my birth mother's death. I confronted my mom, and it was one fucked-up conversation. She'd always known something was odd about me, and when I told her about my ability, she didn't hide the lie anymore. My mom still doesn't know about our world; most humans can't wrap their heads around the fact that supernaturals exist. *I* didn't even know this world existed until much later. Anyhow, my explanation only confused her. But she was open with me and confessed everything about my birth. Maybe it was the guilt of carrying the secret for so many years."

This was harder to talk about than he'd expected. Most Breed didn't associate with humans unless they had to, but Kane didn't share that mindset. He didn't see them as that much different outside of a few extra abilities the Breed had. Yet, something as simple as his upbringing had made his life so damn complicated.

"Don't stop, Kane. Tell me what happened." She squeezed his hand reassuringly, and before he knew it, he was telling her a story that no one else had ever been privy to.

"Around the time I was born, my dad—the man who raised me—was a truck driver and finishing his route on the East

Coast. Mom went through her pregnancy living alone, and one night she went into premature labor in an empty parking lot behind a warehouse. She hadn't been feeling well all day and was looking for a dealer to give her something to take the edge off. We all knew that Mom was a user; that's something our dad threw in her face a lot during their fights. The pains started coming so fast that she had to slide into the backseat and deliver it herself. The baby was born dead. She got scared and wrapped it in a bag and put it in a trash bin."

"Oh my God." Caroline gasped as she sat up beside him. "That's awful. Why did she do something like that?"

"She was scared the cops would blame her for the baby being stillborn because of her addiction. I don't know what kind of shit was going on in the cosmos that night, but when she got back to the car, there I was, swaddled in a blanket in the front seat. So she took me home and pretended that I was hers. All those years, she wondered if maybe it was just a hallucination from being high on whatever she had been taking that day to get through the pain."

"No one found her baby?"

"There was a blip in the news about a pregnant woman they'd found dead, whose body had gone missing, but nothing about a baby."

"Cleaners," Caroline said.

She was right. The Breed never allowed one of their own to be taken by humans; they had inside men who worked in hospitals and law enforcement, disposing of all evidence to keep our secret safe from humans. That evidence also included bodies.

"Yeah. She didn't mention if anyone had found *her* baby in the trash. Probably not. I'll never know what happened with my real parents or why I lived. Mom never told a soul, but my dad knew I wasn't his. I didn't look anything like them. He never said anything until I left home; he just disowned me and said that I wasn't even his son. I guess he thought that my mom had an affair, and sometimes I wonder if that's why he made her life a living hell. Someone murdered my real mother. That's what I lifted from the bloodstain on the blanket. Death never leaves; it sticks around like an invisible fingerprint waiting to be dusted."

"So you grew up without knowing any Sensors?" she asked.

"I grew up thinking I was one fucked-up human until I hit my late teens and met another Breed." He stroked his left hand down her arm very slowly, secretly taking pleasure in being able to feel the soft skin of a woman without any pain involved. "You ask a lot of questions, Caroline."

The soft feel of a woman's body sank against him like a security blanket.

"I like it when you say my name," she said decidedly. "No one ever calls me that."

Kane looked down, taking a deep breath. This reality was so

vivid that he couldn't get over how real she felt in his arms. Her scent reminded him of wildflowers on a hot summer morning.

"You have a pretty name, and I think you need to drop the Carrie nickname. I didn't like that movie."

"Then you can call me Caroline, but no one else can." Her fingers traced small circles on his stomach, and he sucked in a sharp breath. Kane loved the sound of her voice, and having her wedged against him made it feel like she belonged there.

"How much time do you think I have left?" she asked wistfully.

"Decades."

Kane tenderly stroked her cheek with the back of his fingers. It was a gesture he had always denied himself, but one that never escaped his attention when he watched the physical interaction between other couples. He'd always wanted to be one of those guys who could cup a woman's face in his hands, stroking her cheeks with his thumbs while kissing her hard and slow. Unfortunately, the gloves made it an impossibility to indulge in such fantasies.

Her pupils dilated when she looked up at him, and his eyes instinctively dragged down to her lips. Kane thought about leaning in and finding out how soft her mouth really was, and if it tasted as sweet as it looked. His mind swam with provocative images of kissing her so deeply that she would know to whom she belonged. He gave himself a snap with a mental rubber band and discouraged the thought. He'd never sought that kind of claim on a woman, and it didn't make sense to allow that idea into his head now, given the circumstances. *It's not real*, he kept telling himself, *and she's not mine.*

He admired the curve of her neck and licked his lips as he thought about pressing a kiss against her shoulder.

There he went again, distracting himself.

A laugh rumbled in his chest like thunder. It was a good thing that she couldn't read his mind.

"What's so funny?" She smiled a little, waiting for his answer.

"Nothing. I was just thinking about how we met."

CHAPTER 5

NO ONE HAD EVER USED her name in the intimate way that Kane did, and Carrie loved the way the vowels rolled off his tongue. He carried an air of confidence about him that was attractive—one that had nothing to do with his looks and everything to do with being an honorable man that you could count on to do the right thing. Kane didn't have the body of a fighter, but he had taut ropes of muscle in his arms and an air of assuredness whenever he spoke. Carrie felt protected in his strong arms.

Safe. As if he could keep anything bad from happening to her.

He also smelled good, which didn't make any sense. They were inside *her* head, so only things derived from her own memories should be detectable. Yet when she buried her nose against his chest, his scent was dark and heady. It wrapped around her mind and body as if it had complete control.

The room chilled, and she curled around his warm body like a python.

Kane was more than a flame; he was a torch in the darkness.

It seemed like hours had crawled by when he left her alone again to try to wake her up. What if he never came back? Who could blame him? Trapped inside the head of a soon-to-be dead girl sounded like a great way to spend an evening. Maybe it *was* too much for her to expect such intimate companionship from a stranger.

Watching the dwindling hours of her life tick away with every breath was agony. At least she didn't own any pets to worry about; the only things that depended on her were a few ferns. Then the thought of Jesse looking for her gifts on the balcony made Carrie sad. The longer she thought about it, the madder she became.

Mad and scared. It was the kind of fear that made a person feel insignificant and powerless. At least she'd been able to fight against the man who tried to take her life—but how could she fight inevitability?

Carrie paced the quiet room and tried to listen beyond the walls. The air licked at her skin like a sheet of ice. She slid down the wall and pulled her legs up, hugging her knees.

Alone. Kane had left her and she was going to sit in here by herself until she went crazy or slowly died. She hadn't felt so abandoned since her father's disappearance.

"Caroline? Could you hear me?"

Tears spilled from her eyes when Kane reappeared.

"No. It isn't working, and you keep leaving me." Shivers embraced her like a cold lover.

Kane's brow pinched in the middle, leaving a deep crease. When he disappeared again, Carrie put her head down on her knees and squeezed her legs tightly. What if she couldn't wake up?

Several minutes elapsed. When Kane returned, his arms wrapped around her like two protective shields. He wasn't just holding her; he was enveloping her with his warmth.

"Since we're in *your* head, why don't you imagine a couch to sit on with lots of blankets? You don't have to freeze to death in here; build a fire."

She loved his voice; the rich vibration when he spoke made it easy to believe anything he said. It soothed her like a crackling fire, and she wanted him to keep talking until the madness in her head disappeared.

Carrie hadn't thought of that. Something that large would take far more effort than the smaller items. She closed her eyes and concentrated. When she finally looked up, a couch had materialized on the right side of the room. Plush, brown, and dressed up with her favorite beige blanket.

He stood up with his arms around her, and while it was awkward, Carrie didn't complain. She tucked her arms snugly against his chest and relished the way he held on to her. The link with Kane wasn't just in his touch—their connection was on a deeper level now. They had shared private secrets that people would only tell a close friend or a lover. This was the darkest time in her life, and a simple twist of fate kept her from having to experience the impending darkness all alone.

Kane lifted her up, and she giggled, feet dangling helplessly off the ground. He began to sit on the couch, but when he glanced hesitantly over his shoulder, he set her back down. Their lover's embrace wasn't going to make this easy.

His throat cleared. "How are we going to—?"

Carrie was a born problem solver, so she pushed him down. They both collapsed onto the couch, knocking heads and laughing. Once her giggles subsided, she climbed on top of his lap. The only comfortable way to sit was to straddle him with her arms wrapped around his neck.

"Let me go back and hold your hand or something," he said. His breath hitched when she slid her legs up and her head nestled into his neck. Carrie's dress rode up, revealing her left thigh, but she didn't care. His hands were already where they needed to be. "You can wrap up in the blanket, and we don't have to do this. I don't have to be holding you so…"

"Stay with me, Kane. Just for a little while."

His body generated heat like the sun, and she relaxed, rubbing her nose against his neck. He groaned and tightened his hold.

"I covered your body with a warm blanket," he said absently. "Maybe that'll help."

"It won't matter," Carrie murmured. "It's not my body that's cold. Can you tell me another story to pass the time?"

"No. No more about me. You already know too much, and it's not the kind of shit you need to hear right now. They're not happy stories. Why don't you tell me why a pretty girl like you isn't married?"

She snorted against his neck. "My right hook?"

They both laughed.

"That would be a selling point for me," he said. "So why no kids or family?"

She shrugged a little. "You know how it is. Sensors don't want a defective wife."

"You're *not* defective," he growled in a low voice.

That warmed Carrie more than she had expected. No one had ever stuck up for her disability before, nor had any guy looked at her the way Kane did.

"What's the use of being what I am if I can't even transmit anything? Sure, I can experience all I want, but there's no exchange," she pointed out. "I wouldn't have wanted to use my gifts to make money trading, but in the bedroom… you know how it is."

Kane shifted his hip, and she sat up to look at him. A ruddy color darkened his cheeks, and she caught a spectacular glimpse of the coppery orange in the center of his hazel eyes.

"I've never been with another Sensor," he admitted, averting his eyes to the left. "Not the way you're supposed to be with joined hands and sharing. I have conditions when it comes to sex."

"What conditions?"

"Gloves."

Carrie licked her lips. "But you're not wearing any."

"Yeah," he said with a short laugh. "I have to touch you to be here. I normally wear gloves all the time—I can't deal with physical contact because it's too painful to tolerate. I sure as hell don't want to experience any of that in the bedroom or it might kill my sex life for good. I've never been able to touch someone without sensory overload, not until you."

"Sure, hit on the coma victim," she said, winking at him.

His brow slanted down in the most devious way. It was naughty and good-humored all at once. "I'm not even able to touch a woman when she's sleeping, I'm *that* sensitive. Something is so different about you, Caroline."

"I'm a dead transmitter; that's why you aren't picking up anything."

His nose touched her cheek as he leaned forward and drew in a deep breath. "Then explain why it is that I can smell cookies. I should also mention that your right hook left quite a mark on my face, and you know what else? My balls are still throbbing from your target practice."

Carrie's face heated.

She'd never done anything like that before. In real life, she was a mellow person—not the aggressive bitch that Kane must have thought she was. But after some maniac had tried to end her life, Carrie had learned how to get in touch with her primal side.

"Don't do that," he whispered against her cheek. "Your blush makes me feel guilty, like I did something wrong. I'm not a bad guy, not until tonight. I deserve to go to jail for what I did." Kane lowered his eyes remorsefully and pulled back.

"You don't have to talk about it, Kane. But don't you dare feel guilty for saving my life."

It wasn't much of a life to save, but what she didn't tell him was how grateful she felt that he was here. She wasn't alone, and that comforted her.

Carrie would have given anything to be sitting in her living room, flipping through TV channels. She'd never again complain about the high price of her electric bill or the Shifter with the funny mustache who used to hit on her at work. The thought crossed her mind about how she'd always wanted children. Being a mom was something that was in her blood; she was so good with kids, but it would be impossible unless she met a careless Sensor who didn't wear protection. Who was she kidding? They *all* wore protection. No Sensor wanted to take the chance of having a child if the woman wasn't the right match in regards to having superior abilities, and a Sensor was the only kind of Breed that she could have children with.

"Caroline? Where are you?"

A tear crossed her cheek and trailed beneath her chin. Kane

had such a beautiful face for a man, sharp edges around the jaw and the kind of hair she wanted to mess up with her fingers. It was so easy to imagine waking up beside him in the morning; he had the kind of relaxed face that she would have loved to see smiling as he stretched and opened his eyes. Did he snore? Was he the kind of man who made love at first light, or the kind who got up to brush his teeth first? So many things that Carrie would never know. She wanted to kiss him but wiped her face instead.

He offered her a charming smirk. "Why don't you tell me what your favorite color is?"

"Yellow." She sniffed and wiped her nose. "What about you?"

His eyes flicked down for a moment. "Blue," he finally said. "What's your favorite dessert?"

She laughed and patted his chest. "This is like a date gone wrong. Do you really want to know this stuff, or are you just killing time?" Her fingers slid up to his neck, and he flinched.

"I want to know," he said, looking her straight in the eye. It made her stomach flutter nervously, but she decided to play along.

"Strawberry shortcake, no cream, but I like powdered sugar sprinkled on top. What's yours?"

"Hmm," he pondered, as if he'd never given it much thought. "I guess nachos."

"That's *not* a dessert!" she protested.

"Oh?" His eyebrow arched. "Then what is it?"

"An appetizer. Dessert has to be something sweet."

His lip twitched, and he cleared his throat. "Well then, I guess I'd have to say trail mix."

"You're impossible!" She tried to pull away, but he gathered her up in his arms and waggled his handsome brow.

"And *you* are beautiful," he said in a soft and serious voice.

When Kane leaned forward, he tested her mouth with a brush of his lips. The moment they touched, tiny sparks ignited across her body, and a surge of desire swelled inside her. His tongue stroked her bottom lip, and then he suddenly stopped. They were a breath apart, staring at one another. The tension was electric, and she swallowed nervously, looking at the man she had just met. A man she was contemplating kissing inside her head. Was she nuts? Then again, what did it really matter? It wasn't as if any of this was real, and God, how she wanted to run her fingers through his hair and tangle it.

"Sorry," he said in a heated voice, averting his eyes.

The moment was crushed like a cigarette beneath a dirty boot. Carrie traced her finger along her lower lip. *Maybe he changed his mind because I'm not normal,* she thought. It wouldn't have been the first time, and maybe that had been nothing more than a pity kiss.

She snapped back at him, suddenly irritated. "Will you at least call someone to get my body when I die?"

His face paled, and a moment later, Kane was gone.

Kane ran into the kitchen and swung the fridge door open to look for a beer. Anything to dull the guilt. A bottle of ketchup tipped over in the door, and the cold air made the hairs on his arms rise up. Reality slammed into him like a hard fist—if he didn't hurry his ass up and figure something out, this girl was going to die. Who was he kidding? Not even a Relic could save her in the condition she was in, but it didn't make him feel any less shitty for not trying. Caroline's comment wasn't a request; it was an accusation that he was doing nothing to help her.

Loud voices in the living room almost made him leap out of his socks. When he peered around the corner, he blew out a slow breath. The television was on an automatic timer. The clock on the microwave was blinking five in the morning, and he was in the house of a serial killer. Kane wiped his bicep across his forehead, holding it steady for a few minutes while he closed his eyes and regained his composure.

His throat was dry, so he flipped on the faucet and filled a clean glass with water that tasted of chlorine. Three swallows polished off the glass and he set it in the sink, listening to his stomach growl like an animal. Here he was, wishing that a steak would appear. Meanwhile, that poor girl was suffering from a head injury.

Spatters of blood on his shirt caught his attention when he

brushed a hand over them. A faint red glow emanated from his fingertips. The stains were dark and hardly noticeable, but his hands lit up on contact. That was part of his Sensor abilities; when he picked up strong emotions, there was an energy glow. The emotional content of the murder was all over him, and Kane shuddered, wanting to strip out of his shirt. He began polishing the handles of everything he'd touched, knowing that his imprints were all over the house. Fingerprints, hairs, molecules, emotions.

Jesus.

On his way back to the bedroom, he stopped cold in his tracks. A blond news anchor with heavy mascara spoke in rushed words about an unidentified body found in an alley. They had a police sketch on the screen and provided a number to call with any information. Time was not about to hang out, have a few drinks, and be on his side. How could he check up on his little sis and send her money if he was locked up in Breed jail? He already felt like a shitty older brother. He hadn't visited Sunny in over a year and had even missed her last birthday, which was a first.

Kane went back into the bedroom and patted Caroline's cheek.

"Enough of this. I want you to open your eyes and look at me. Caroline, can you hear me in there?"

His fingers tested the wound on her head. The bone didn't feel crushed, but there could be a crack or bleeding inside that he couldn't see. Why the fuck hadn't he become a doctor? It wasn't an uncommon profession among Sensors since they were able to feel the exact symptoms of the patient, but who the hell wants to feel pain all day?

The raw flesh around her gaping wound made his stomach turn.

Kane rushed into the hall and tore apart the bathroom until he found some gauze and one of those ACE bandages. With an armload of supplies, he returned to the room and pressed a cotton ball against the rim of the peroxide bottle, then gently dabbed the blood away and cleaned the wound. He watched her serene expression as she took shallow breaths. Kane opened the bedside drawer in search of a tissue. Instead, what he found was a bottle of superglue.

He'd read stories about doctors using superglue to seal wounds—even in the Vietnam War. There was no way he was going to try to sew a needle through there. Shit, he couldn't even sew a button on his shirt. Kane chewed on his bottom lip for a minute while staring at the tube.

It didn't take long for him to make a decision. Kane put his gloves back on and carefully unscrewed the narrow cap. He had a good angle and applied it along the edge of the cut, pressing it together tightly. Infections could be nasty, and he had to think on the fly. The cut was right on the hairline and easy to see. She'd have an ugly scar, but at least it wouldn't be on her face.

The bandage wasn't the best idea, but he managed to get it on tight after two attempts, wrapping it so that he could see her eyes.

"Don't worry," he said. "I'm going to fix you up. And when you snap out of this, you're going to kick my ass for gluing your head together." Wasn't *that* the truth? He almost cringed at the thought.

Kane bit down on the tip of his right glove and pulled it off. His fingers itched to touch her, and he wondered if it was a good idea to keep leaving Caroline alone.

She needed a healer. He ran into a lot of different Breeds working for a delivery service, but Kane could never tell which ones were the Relics. Many were healers or consultants by trade because of the specific knowledge they retained and passed down genetically to their descendants. They spent their lives acquiring more information about the Breeds that their family specialized in treating. He didn't know how that shit worked, but nothing ceased to amaze him anymore. If he knew where one lived, he could leave Caroline on the Relic's doorstep.

Yeah. In broad daylight, leave a dying woman in front of someone's door. *Real sensitive.*

He cursed under his breath and pinched his earlobe. A delicate gold necklace around her neck caught his eye—the chain was so thin that he almost missed it. The pendant or charm must have slid around her neck, so he reached for it with his bare hand, forgetting about their link.

Then he was back in her private room.

Caroline faced him with her back to the window. The contact between them felt so natural. Her hair captured the light, and a few delicate strands floated carelessly. As he cupped the nape of her neck with his hand, that possessive feeling surged through him again.

Then the little charm slid forward and stopped his heart from beating.

"What's wrong?" She looked down at what captured his interest. "Don't you like it? I wear it all the time even though I'm not fond of gold."

"Why an anchor?" Kane's words came out in a raspy voice. He didn't even notice that he'd been holding his breath.

"I don't know," she said with uncertainty. "I saw it in a store years ago, and even though money was tight… I just had to have it." She touched it with the tip of her finger and dropped her hand. "Maybe it just reminds me not to get swept away in all the bad stuff that happens. I know, it sounds cheesy." She shrugged her shoulders. "But it's one of my most favorite things."

He admired her magnificent shoulders, round and confident with all those tiny sun-kissed freckles. Caroline's eyes were wide and pale brown, matching the radiant color of her hair. It wasn't just the physical traits that made her attractive, but the way she used them. Her eyes glittered with emotion, and her mouth was nothing less than temptation. The moment she parted her lips—so yielding and responsive—he knew he wanted to kiss her.

Despite the fact that she'd tried to kill him, Kane's entire body lit up like an inferno at the idea of her soft body beneath his, smelling her hair, tasting her lips, touching her skin, and hearing his name on her tongue.

"Lift up my shirt," he said.

Her eyes widened.

"Just do it," he said with a reassuring nod.

Caroline pinched the ends of his black cotton shirt and slowly drew it up, revealing his firm abs. His job wasn't an easy one, but all that heavy lifting and time spent outside left him with a toned body. It didn't belong to a bodybuilder, but he could hold his own.

Maybe it was the way she splayed her fingers across his stomach or the wild excitement in her eyes, but Kane stepped *closer*.

Just a little.

"Oh Kane, you're so beautiful," she said, desire clinging to her words.

God, that almost unraveled him completely.

He stroked his thumb across the nape of her neck in slow movements as she admired him. It was intense to watch her appraise his body; her eyes soaked in every inch of him like a sponge, and she was dripping with admiration.

When the shirt was halfway up his chest, he leaned forward. "Lift it up all the way, Caroline. I want you to see all of me."

She obeyed, pulling his shirt over his head until it was stretched behind his neck. Suddenly her breath caught.

Kane's eyes hooded when her finger traced around the dark pattern on his left pec. It was a tattoo of an anchor that he'd gotten on his twentieth birthday.

He'd gone in with his buddies with the intention of getting a dagger or something cool, but when he thumbed through the design book, his eyes stopped on the page with an anchor. What had compelled him to get that damn thing he couldn't explain, even to this day. Tattoos were a personal mark and most had a story behind them, but Kane had no valid reason why he refused to leave the shop that day without that anchor inked on his chest. It was the only tattoo on his body.

Was it fate, or coincidence?

"You're wearing my anchor," she whispered. Kane stepped forward until the fullness of her breasts molded against him.

There was no asking for permission, because her body gave it completely. Caroline widened her legs, and he slid his right knee between them, feeling the delicious warmth. His fingers pressed against the back of her neck and he kissed her hard. There was no buildup or tiny pecks to start lighting the fireworks; it was the big show. Their mouths moved hungrily as they tasted and discovered each other. When her lips parted and allowed his tongue entrance, he moaned.

Caroline made the sweetest gasp, and he hiked up her pretty dress and ran his gloved hand across her thigh. His tongue pushed in deeper, and desire coiled in his belly.

"Hm-mm," she murmured in protest. The kiss broke, and her fingers tugged at his left glove. "Take this off. I want to feel your hands on me, Kane."

She did more than ask; she removed the glove herself and tossed it to the floor. The cool air touched his damp palm, and when she guided his hand back to her silky thigh, he nearly lost it. Lascivious thoughts spilled in his mind as if an inkwell had tipped over.

"Touch me," she begged.

Kane grew rigid at the idea of her saying that over and over again. He felt so inexperienced, enjoying the texture of her smooth thigh against his virgin palm. The kiss was smoldering, creating such palpable warmth that it spread across his chest and shot straight down to his groin. He groaned, and Caroline rubbed her leg against his while his mind swam with images of them undressing each other.

"You don't want this," he said against her mouth. "I'm no good for you."

She wasn't listening as her kiss moved like fire burning away the edges of paper, and Kane was about to become a pile of ash. He loved women, but he'd never felt unworthy of one until now. This one—she was special—she was too good to be with someone like him.

He cupped her face. "You're killing me, angel," Kane said in a strangled voice.

Caroline's fingers clawed across his tattoo, and her tongue pushed deep into his mouth. So deep that everything male within him stirred.

That was it. All sense of control was gone.

Kane reached down and lifted her leg, sliding her onto the window ledge. Caroline wrapped her long legs around his waist, and her back pressed hard against the glass. One of her sandals fell off and clapped on the floor below.

"Make a bed appear," he growled against her mouth.

Out of breath, she replied, "It's not working anymore. I can't do it."

The button on his jeans popped open, and he sucked in his stomach at the feel of her cool knuckles against his skin. Her fingers were only an inch away from a hard ache that demanded to know her in the most intimate way. She slowly kissed her way around his neck and he let out a hard sigh—the kind of sound that a man makes before he loses himself to passion. Those creamy thighs were so soft against his rough fingers, and he slid them beneath her dress, feeling the line of her panties. Kane wanted to commit her body to memory with his hands.

When she made a soft moan, he scraped his cheek against her jaw, breathing hard across her shoulder.

It wasn't right. None of this. Trying to take a woman in her own mind while she was lying unconscious with a head injury, the fact that he was too chickenshit to call a real doctor for help, and even worse was that she was letting him.

"No," he said, creating distance.

Seeing her lips swollen from their kiss and her flushed chest made it harder to deny this woman. "We can't do this. I need to go find someone who can help you."

"Don't you dare leave me!" she said, gripping the shirt behind his shoulders and pulling him close. Fear trembled in her eyes, which were glimmering with tears that sprang from them.

"Why did he do this to me?" she cried. Passion broke into pain, etched in every line and contour of her face. Caroline shook her head, and a hair stuck to her lip. "This isn't fair! I *hate* him for what he did to me," she hissed, choking through sobs. "I'm asking you to stay here with me. Please, Kane, keep me warm until it's over. Don't let me be in the dark alone." The last words broke off.

And broke him.

Hearing her acceptance of death sliced through his chest like an unmerciful sword. Unrelenting sobs reddened her cheeks, and she wept. It was like a cold shower to see her grimace with hopelessness, unable to keep her eyes open as they welled with tears. Death was hunting Caroline, and he couldn't do a damn thing about it.

"I'm not leaving you." He kissed her wet lashes and wiped the tears from her cheeks with the pad of his left thumb. "Don't cry, angel. We're going to stay right here, and everything's going to be all right. You hear me? I'm not letting anything bad happen to you. You're safe," he said, kissing away her salty tears.

Her skin was cool against his lips, and she closed her eyes, accepting his offer.

"I'll be okay if you promise not to leave me," she said, wiping her nose with the back of her hand. Caroline smiled. "I bet I look like a hot mess; I hate crying."

Her brown eyes rose to meet his, and he felt a flutter in the pit of his stomach.

"You're beautiful," he said under his breath. And he meant it. She was truly the most beautiful woman he'd ever known.

The same hand that had cut a man's throat just hours earlier was now holding a life that would slip through his own fingers like tiny grains of sand. Kane was faced with making a choice, and each came with a consequence that would wreck him forever. Staying meant that she would die, and leaving meant that she would do it alone.

"You have my word that I won't leave you," he said in a thick voice. "I'll stay for as long as you can tolerate me."

She snorted, and he lifted her from the window with one arm and set her small feet down on the floor. Kane leaned closer and buried his face in the crook of her neck. Caroline smelled the way a woman should, and she held him fiercely, as if they'd always known each other. He shuffled his clumsy feet to the left and back to the right, attempting to dance with her. She leaned into him, pressing her ear against his pounding heart.

"You're a terrible dancer," she said, laughing softly against his chest.

"Maybe you can teach me. The last time I did this was in the eighth grade. Sarah McGuire seemed to think that I had mad skills."

"Did she now?"

Caroline sniffed a few times, and he smoothed his hand across her back.

"Keep your mind off all the bad stuff because it's not going to happen," he assured her. "It takes time to heal. Just live in this moment with me, and I'll take care of everything. Let's go sit down, and you can tell me all about the men in your life who you've whacked over the head with kitchen utensils."

She laughed, and it pleased him to know he could make her smile. Caroline rested her cheek against his bare chest and wiped her tears across his anchored heart.

CHAPTER 6

KANE TOOK A SEAT ON the couch and pulled Caroline onto his lap. She scooted down low and sat sideways, her left cheek resting on his shoulder. Her hand splayed across his heart, and nothing was more intimate than the idea of her feeling every beat. His right hand still cupped the back of her neck, but he didn't care about his discomfort. He peered over his left shoulder and glared at her feet. One was missing a shoe that had fallen off moments ago, but she might as well have been barefoot.

"Take my socks off and put them on. Go on, do as I say."

Caroline bent over and removed his thick, white socks. She put them on and pulled each one up as high as it would go on her slender legs.

"They're still toasty warm," she said with a faded sigh, leaning into his arms. He looked into her big brown eyes, and her mouth quirked. "You have *really* big feet."

"Well, you know what they say about that," he suggested,

wanting to smack himself in the forehead as soon as the words left his mouth.

"Yep. Big shoes. I once dated a guy whose feet were so small he could have worn my high heels." She laughed, and it was a beautiful sound—like wind chimes on a summer morning. "That was back in high school. Hopefully he hit a growth spurt after I broke up with him."

"So you were a little heartbreaker," he teased, feeling her smile against his neck. Kane stroked a swath of hair from Caroline's face, allowing him to see her better. To touch her beautiful skin and not feel obliterated by emotions was so liberating that all he wanted to *do* was touch her. Sensors experienced life through their hands, and it was the one thing Kane had always denied himself.

With his fingers, he learned more about Caroline. The smooth skin on the back of her earlobe told him that her ears weren't pierced. She had the softest hands, and she wore clear polish on her short fingernails. No frills, and he liked that. There was also a ticklish spot behind her knee. Each time he brushed his finger across that soft patch of skin, she jerked her leg and it made him smile.

"Do you date much?" She arched a brow.

"Not really."

"Liar," she sang.

He pursed his lips. "Here and there whenever I meet someone, I guess. I don't go out with Sensors anymore because they don't get… this," he said, lifting his left hand. But his glove was still on the floor by the window. Kane squeezed his fingers into a fist out of habit.

"Do you always wear gloves?"

He grunted an affirmative.

"I think that's what your problem is, Kane." Caroline moved to sit up, and it stretched out his right arm. "We have a power, and if you never use it—" She pressed her finger on her lower lip in thought. "It's like when you're outside in the hot sun, and the pool sounds like a great idea. You check the temperature and it's ninety, which isn't much lower than your body temperature. But the minute you put your toe in the water, it feels like ice. It's shockingly cold, and that's why people always tell you to jump in. The water is your gift, Kane. You keep avoiding the pool, and every time you put your foot in the water, you get scared by the temperature. You don't need to acclimate and slowly get used to it. Once you jump in, it won't be so bad."

Kane tried to look away, but Caroline got a firm grip on his jaw and turned his head forward.

"Maybe you *are* more sensitive than most of us, but completely avoiding touch will only make it worse."

She had a point. But that would mean physical contact, and Kane just wasn't a touchy-feely kind of guy. What was he supposed to do, hang out at the bar and fondle every woman who sat beside him? Not that he hadn't thought about it.

A lot.

Kane had fantasized about what it would feel like to run his bare hands all over a woman's body. The sensitive skin of her inner thigh, the smooth curve at the base of her spine, the delicate skin on her breast, the flat of her stomach—places he'd tasted with his mouth but never touched with his hands. Not until this woman had come into his life.

"You're right," he agreed. "Maybe I'll give it a try someday." He looked away for a moment and then changed the subject. "Have you ever been in love?"

He knew a woman like her must have dated, but had a man ever claimed her as his own? Part of him was a little bit jealous about that. Kane had never been in a serious relationship where the L-word had come out of his mouth, and he didn't know what possessed him to ask. He didn't think commitment was in his genetic makeup, and it had never seemed like a big deal. Even his sister shared the same cynical outlook about love. Perhaps it was his dysfunctional childhood and the poor example shown by his parents that carved the man he had become. Stuff like that messes with your head whether you realize it or not.

"Once."

When she didn't speak anymore, he brushed her hair aside and ran his thumb over her eyebrow. "Tell me about the loser who let you go."

Her eyes looked up wistfully. "He was a human. I was

young and didn't know any better. I thought it wouldn't matter who I dated. Boy, was I wrong."

An unsettling feeling shifted within him. "What do you mean?"

She wet her lips and traced a finger over his tattoo. "I met Tommy at the grocery store of all places." A thoughtful smile curved up her cheek. "I pulled an orange out of a fancy pyramid and sent a dozen of them rolling to the floor."

Kane laughed. He could see that image in his mind so vividly.

"Tommy was the manager, and he was so nice about not making me feel like an idiot. He was five years older than me and just a really nice guy. We didn't live together, but we dated for about five months."

"That serious?"

She cleared her throat a little. "Yeah, it was getting serious."

"Did you tell him what you were?"

"I wanted to, but never got around to it. Plus, I was scared that he might tell others about us and I'd get in trouble. Everything was so perfect, and I didn't want to spoil anything. Then my boss found out. This was my old job when I used to work at a café."

Kane nodded and glared at the darkening window.

"Tommy came into the shop a lot, and my boss started getting into my business. He was a Shifter, and you know how territorial some of them are. A wolf, no less." Caroline's voice saddened as she recollected something long ago. "He didn't like it one bit and threatened to kill Tommy if we didn't stop seeing each other. I was scared because every time I went out with him, it felt like someone was following us. My boss was serious and said he'd follow through with it even if I quit working there. I couldn't report him because that would have been slander. Was I supposed to wait around until one day Tommy disappeared? I had no choice."

"Your boyfriend didn't try to hold on to you?"

She shrugged. "I didn't have a believable reason for breaking up, so I told him what no man wants to hear. That I'd cheated on him. Tommy knew better and called me a liar; he didn't understand. It was the worst thing I've ever done to anyone, and you have no idea how many nights I've wanted to call him and take it all back." Her sigh was a pained one. "God, I said things to him I'll regret for the rest of my life."

Kane's left hand brushed down her arm. "So why don't you call him now?"

"He's married with two kids. What am I going to say to him now that would matter?" As the words left her lips, Caroline shivered.

"Give me your hand," he said, pulling it up to his mouth. He cupped her fingers within his own and blew a heated breath. It reminded him of what they were really doing; this was no date. In reality, both of them were lying in bed together with the early morning sun showering the room with light.

"Better?"

"So much." She stretched out her words and relaxed against him. "Where do you live?"

"Far side of town near a little diner called Coyote Burger. They've got the best damn onion rings."

She gripped his arm and shook it. "Are you serious? I'm right there on the *same* street—just a few blocks up by the gas station. I've never tried their onion rings, but their shakes are to die for. That's where I went tonight to get my dinner."

"No kidding."

"I go there almost every single Friday. Usually I sit in the back next to that crappy old jukebox."

Kane chuckled softly. "Yeah, the one that always plays Willie Nelson songs."

Caroline laughed, and it was a lovely sound—melodic and followed with a sigh. "The owner has a thing for country music, and Willie is his man."

When she rested her head against his chest, he inconspicuously leaned forward and brushed his lips over her soft hair, feeling the back of her neck with his hand and the weight of her body in his lap. Everything was so real.

"Did you know the guy who grabbed you?"

"No," she said, shaking her head. "He came out of nowhere and cornered me in a parking lot."

Kane cursed under his breath.

"I wish we'd met before all this," she said, stroking his arm.

"Although I'm a little shy sometimes and probably wouldn't have said anything to you. I might have just stared at your gorgeous ass over the top of my menu or something like that." She snickered.

"I would have tried to hit on you," he said decidedly. Kane stroked her rosy cheek with the pad of his thumb. "You're so noticeable that everything else isn't. One look and I would have been a goner. You—you're so lovely, Caroline. I might have stuck my foot in my mouth."

"Your big foot," she added.

"Yes, my big foot." He laughed softly. "I'm going to take you there and let you try those onion rings."

Caroline lifted her chin. "I'd like that. Afterward, we can do something fun. What do you like to do?"

Kane suddenly felt nervous—this girl was a gem, and nothing about him was the kind of guy she'd go for. But he played along because it indulged his fantasy. "Nothing you'd be interested in. Concerts, pool… that kind of thing."

"Ah, so what do you think I do for fun?" she asked in a sharp tone. "I don't sit around and read books all day if that's what you're implying."

Kane laughed as she shifted angrily in his lap. "Never said such a thing, angel. I just don't see girls like you in places where I hang out."

"I like fun," she huffed. Then a wide smile spread across her face. "How do you feel about museums?"

When he groaned and stretched out his legs, she pinched his side and laughed triumphantly. Their bodies settled together once more, and the only sound in that quiet room was the two of them breathing in rhythm.

Carrie loved the feeling of being encased in Kane's arms—she felt as if nothing in the world mattered. Kane wasn't the kind of guy who would normally give her the time of day. Guys like him never hit on girls like her. He was one of those bad boys with a thunderous sex life—the one who struts into a café and leans against the counter on his elbows, flirting with the girl behind the register while he takes his time deciding which flavor of coffee he wants. He might casually look around the room to soak up the admiring glances with those beautiful eyes.

And wow, those eyes. She'd never seen anything so captivating as the way his eyes looked when they fell over her body. His gaze was more than carnal desire—it was reverent. Carrie was always a sucker for a smile, but the way he looked at her made her blush.

"What are you thinking about?" he asked. "You got quiet all of a sudden." His hand cupped her arm and lightly stroked it, warming her completely.

What she wanted to tell him was that she was thinking

about the way he called her angel. It was a name reserved for someone close to your heart. What a silly thought. Carrie took a cleansing breath. He smelled so good. How was it possible that she could smell him?

"Angel?"

Her heart skipped. "I was just thinking about how you should have kids."

"What would make you say something like that?" He snorted.

Carrie reached up and tenderly brushed her hand across his brow. This time he didn't flinch. Maybe it was the fact that none of this was real that made it easier to be affectionate. "You need to give those beautiful eyes to someone."

And that's when his heart began to pound against her chest. Immediately, Carrie felt like such an idiot. She was practically throwing herself at his feet with silly nonsense that…

"Maybe I'd rather give them to you," he said in a raspy voice. "A guy like me? I'm not someone a kid could look up to."

Carrie rested her hand across his tattoo. He didn't seem to care that his shirt was still pulled behind his head, and she didn't mention it. "I think you're wrong. Plus, I'm sure there are lots of women who would love to make babies with you."

Kane rocked with laughter. Carrie loved the way the shadows played on his features and how his Adam's apple moved when he laughed. She wanted to run her fingers through his disheveled hair.

His grip tightened around the nape of her neck. "You make me sound like a playboy. I'm not that kind of guy," he said as his chuckles faded.

"Oh, *please.*"

He narrowed his eyes, tilting his head to one side. "Care to explain?"

She twisted her mouth. "You're the guy who can get any girl he wants, but you don't give girls like me the time of day."

"Maybe it's because I don't like rejection."

Carrie leaned back and stared at his mouth. He wet his lips with his tongue and pursed them, studying her as if he was trying to figure something out. *Rejection?* Now he was really mocking her.

"What makes you think I'd reject you?"

He arched a brow and smirked. "The lump on my head? Or maybe the bruised knuckles," he said, holding up his hand and looking at them. "I'm not sure which. Could be my aching balls."

She laughed so hard that she had to curl up against him to hide her face. Maybe she would have judged him harshly, afraid that a guy like him would break her heart. The thought made her a little sad, thinking about missed opportunities when she could have easily gotten out of her comfort zone and actually talked to a guy who was looking in her direction. Carrie had closed herself off, and maybe part of that was the residual pain from losing the one man that meant everything to her.

"I'm sorry," she said.

"For?"

Silence stretched between them.

"What I said about your name. I didn't mean it. You *are* someone important, Kane. Don't let anyone ever tell you differently."

He drew invisible circles on her knee with his finger but didn't say a word. She felt horrible for the way she had treated him at first. What did she really know about Kane, aside from the fact that he was a complete stranger trying to help her? That spoke volumes.

Especially given her past. After her father disappeared, Carrie had been thrown into temporary housing. There weren't many other kids there, but it was no different from an orphanage. Unfortunately, Sensors weren't big on adopting, so they kept unwanted children in a facility until they were old enough to find a job. Because of her disability, the workers had treated her unkindly. It was hard enough having to cope with the loss of her father, but to be treated like some kind of leper? There was no other family; her grandmother had died a couple of years earlier. Carrie had sensed her father had never recovered from the loss of her mother, who'd died in childbirth.

There'd been many sleepless nights when Carrie had gazed at the stars through the dusty window and wished someone would come to her rescue. Maybe that's why she was a hopeless romantic, always watching those sappy movies and wanting to experience the burning passion of a great love. Just once. The kind that was reckless and filled in all the cracks that had left her broken.

"I miss my dad," she said in a quiet breath.

"He died?"

She lightly patted Kane's chest. "I don't know. I was young when he went missing. My dad was a decent man—not affectionate, but he always read me stories when I was little, and he tried his best to make me happy."

"Maybe he'll come back."

"I doubt it," she said. "It's been years. If he was alive and had to remain hidden for some reason, he would have at least sent me a note or something to let me know that he was okay. I just can't believe it's that easy to abandon someone you love."

Kane scooted down in his seat and pulled her legs up, keeping his hand on her thigh. She wasn't aware of anything else but the heat from his palm through her dress. "How old were you?"

"Fifteen. I waited two days before I called law enforcement," she said guiltily. "They don't really do much about missing persons. They said that it's not uncommon among Breed for a killer to dispose of the body so that no evidence will link back to them."

Dammit. Her lip was quivering just thinking about how

insensitive the detectives had been; talking about it opened up all those old feelings. She'd been just a young girl, and that was the day her childhood ended.

Without warning, Kane slowly caressed her cheek with his fingers. They traced down the line of her jaw and she closed her eyes, realizing that he was the man she wanted to wake up next to.

Caroline gently held his hand and stroked his wrist with her fingertips. It was becoming harder for Kane to breathe because of the guilt that sat on his chest like a five-hundred-pound gorilla.

Caroline was a remarkable woman, and he wanted to learn more about her. He wanted to take her out for pancakes and coffee, find out what she did in her spare time, and even watch her fall asleep. He barely knew this woman, and yet she knew him better than anyone else. When someone else sees your secrets, shares your pain, and looks into your soul, it's hard not to feel like the luckiest person on earth.

"Will you remember me, Kane?"

Fuck, he thought, looking away. The darkness shielded his face and hid the tears that branded him a feeling man. The bitch of it was that he couldn't wipe them away because his hands were all hers. He'd never lost anyone close, so death had always been an impersonal fact of life to him.

"Kane?" She sounded afraid.

"Yes," he whispered, still looking away.

Her cool hand slid around the back of his neck. "Look at me. I can't see your face anymore—I need to see you."

He swallowed hard and clenched his jaw, facing her with a stoic expression. The moment she planted her glimmering eyes on him, Kane was ruined. He wanted to see the tiny beauty mark on her cheek and thread his hands through her sunlit hair.

Without thinking, he bent forward and kissed her. It wasn't combustible like before, but slow and simmering. He tasted her in a way that was new and bittersweet. The salt of her tears still stained her lips, and his nose filled with the bloom of wildflowers. The wet sound of their slow kiss filled the darkening room, and he took his time, placing soft pecks on each corner of her mouth. For once, Kane truly knew what it was to enjoy a woman—to savor her so completely that nothing was rushed or forgotten.

When he broke away, she briefly covered his mouth with her hand. "Tell me you love me."

He frowned and shook his head. "What?"

"Just listen for a minute. No man has ever said it to me before—not even Tommy—and I want to hear what it sounds like." Her chin wrinkled as she staved off tears, and it strengthened the bones in her face. She was the reason that warriors wrote poetry.

"Caroline—"

"*Please* do this for me, Kane. It won't mean anything to you, but I need to know what it feels like to hear a man say those words. Let me pretend that I'm leaving something behind. Sure I dated around, but you know how it is. They'd find out the truth and leave pretty quickly, so kids were never in my future. I have no legacy."

"They were clowns. Those men didn't deserve you."

"Yeah, but it would have been nice to be missed."

She leaned in close enough that her nose touched his cheek. "I thought about adopting a human baby, but they would have arrested me. I don't think there's a law against it, but—"

"It wouldn't have been worth going to jail for."

"Maybe it would have." Caroline's voice relaxed, like when you're lying in bed late at night and talking about deep things. She moved her mouth to a spot just beneath his jaw, and he tensed as she kept talking. "One of the best memories I have is baking cookies in my grandma's kitchen. She always wore this blue apron with little yellow flowers and let me taste the first one that came out of the oven while it was warm. Even though she's gone, she's still here because I remember her. That woman lived a long time," Caroline said with a small laugh. "She liked reminding everyone how old she was."

"I'll outlive my human family," Kane said offhandedly.

"I never thought of that." Caroline rested her cheek against his shoulder. He shuddered as her breath tickled his neck. "Maybe you should meet someone and have a few kids."

That stung. For a fleeting moment, his life of delivering packages and sitting around drinking beers dissipated—replaced with visions of Caroline baking in the kitchen and running to give him a kiss. Could he be that kind of man?

"I'm going back to get help. This is fucking ridiculous—me sitting here when I should have taken you to a hospital and hung around to keep an eye on you. No one has to know; we'll let them treat your injuries, and when you wake up, I'll sneak you out of there."

"I'm asking you to stay," she insisted.

Kane shook his head. "No, this isn't right. What the hell am I doing here if I'm not helping you?" The tattoo across his heart burned like a brand.

"You *are* helping me, Kane. You just don't know it. I'm not asking you to miss me; I'm not even asking that you remember me. Just tell me once that you *love* me." Caroline kissed the soft spot on his neck below his Adam's apple. "This is how you can save me. I don't matter to anyone, but this life matters to me. All the things I wanted to do," she said remorsefully. "My body can't be saved. Just do this, Kane. Kiss me and say something that doesn't matter because it won't make a difference to you, but it'll make it easier for me to let go. I won't feel so… alone."

He looked down; their lips were only a breath apart. The

intensity of her stare created a tension that buzzed between them. It was past twilight and the light—*her* light—was almost gone.

She stroked his bristly jaw with her thumbs, whispering against his mouth. "I want to see your eyes when you say it. Just pretend, Kane. Tell me you love me before it ends. I promise no tears, and you can even leave me here if you want. Grant a girl her dying wish?"

Kane licked his dry lips, and his throat constricted. Didn't seem like such a difficult request, except that the words were tumbling around in his mouth like loose marbles. Prickling sensations needled his chest, and a sting of sweat touched his brow. He caught the last flicker of light in her eyes when they went dark, and he felt her no more.

"I love you, Caroline."

Darkness enveloped them, and he could no longer feel her in his arms.

"*I love you, my sweet Kane.*"

His eyes snapped open, and he was sitting up in the bed. Sunshine covered the both of them like a spotlight.

Caroline was gone.

CHAPTER 7

"C AROLINE!" KANE ROARED, STRADDLING HER body and slamming his hands against the mattress on either side of her. "Wake up!"

His heart sped out of control when the connection between them broke. Adrenaline poured through his veins like gasoline, and he leapt off the bed, tilting her head back to begin CPR. It wasn't something he'd ever done before, but the medical shows on television were descriptive enough that the average person could grasp the idea.

After thirty compressions, he placed his mouth on hers and blew a breath into her empty lungs. He searched for a pulse with his fingers.

Nothing.

Kane relentlessly administered a series of breaths, pumping on her chest to force blood through her heart.

"One, two, three, four, five, six, seven," he counted aloud.

Sweat trickled down his temple, and his shoulders stiffened.

Every passing minute was agony as part of him wanted to rush to the phone and call someone—anyone. But he couldn't risk losing one precious second.

When he blew another breath and checked for a pulse, Kane's heart sank into a bottomless pit of despair.

He made bargains in his head that he'd stop all the stupid shit. He'd turn himself in and serve his time. If they ever released him, he would get a better job and do something meaningful with his life. If she'd just breathe on her own again, Kane vowed he would look after her. Even if she wanted nothing to do with him, there would never be a moment's worry in her life for money. He'd work his ass off to make sure she had what she needed.

"Come on, Caroline. I know you can hear me," he shouted. "Wake up and hit me again because I deserve it!"

Twenty minutes? Maybe closer to forty-five. In the silence of the room illuminated by early morning light, Kane collapsed across her lifeless body as the realization hit that Caroline was gone.

He couldn't save her.

His body sagged from the weight of the guilt, and he wiped his brow against his trembling bicep. The only sound was his ragged breath.

No birds sang for her passing, and the breaking dawn honored her with a moment of silence. Caroline had no family to grieve for her, no lover to hold her hand and smooth away her fears, no children to cry themselves to sleep. A lovely girl who'd vibrated with life and so much promise… had slipped through his unworthy fingers.

Fury consumed him and he grimaced, feeling the hot flames of anger scorching his face. He wanted to flip over all the furniture and set the house on fire. Smash every piece of glass, kick in every door, and rip the blinds from the windows. He wanted to go back in time and kick the living shit out of that man until the violence in him quit raging. This beautiful girl had been ripped from the world, torn from his hands, and cast into the darkness by fate.

But when he lifted his head, she anchored him back to his senses.

Her expression was angelic, and he could see the tiny mark on her cheek again. Kane brushed his thumb tenderly over it and leaned closer to her face, pulling away the bandage so he could see her eyes more clearly.

Closed eyes. Ones that should have awakened and filled with the morning light of the sun.

The truth of how he felt about Caroline hadn't sunk in until those three words crossed his lips—words simply meant to offer comfort. But Kane had never said those words to a woman before, not in a way that really meant anything. All Caroline wanted was someone to stay with her in the darkness, talk with her in the silence, and care for her in the solitude.

He should have kissed her.

This was the decision in his life that would break him, the one he would remember in those odd moments when something reminded him of Caroline.

Kane leaned forward, pressing his warm lips against hers. They were cool to the touch. Very lovingly, he delivered a heartfelt kiss.

He felt nothing from her, but for the first time—he felt *everything*. All reason broke away, and tears washed down his jaw and onto her cheeks. No woman had ever broken through his façade and accepted the man that he was.

He spoke in a raspy voice against her face.

"You were wrong, Caroline. You matter. We would have been a pair, you know that? I would have taken you out on a date and showed you off in that dress."

The one still covered in her blood—but that's not how he'd remember it. He'd always see her standing in the spray of sunlight by the window with her tenacious spirit and gentle laugh. Kane wondered if any man in her life had really noticed how beautiful she was. Anything. He'd give *anything* to feel her touch again.

Kane placed the flat of his hand across her chest where the necklace charm had settled across her heart. Nothing could have prepared him for the devastating loss of hope, promise, and a young woman who'd bared her soul to him in the darkest moment of her life.

A burst of pain tore through his heart like a dagger and

ripped him open. Exposed were the lies of all the times he'd told himself that he could never love a woman. Heated tears stung his eyes.

Kane held her cheek with his bare hand, speaking quietly against her lips. Sorrow was the sunlight wrapping them tight, fury was the regret that burned in his heart, and tender was his kiss. He honored her with memory.

It was all he had to give.

"I meant it, Caroline, I *do* love you. No other woman will ever matter. You're in *my* head now, and as long as I'm alive, I'm going to remember you, angel. *Always.*"

The sunlight warmed his arms, as if trying to offer a consoling touch, but he felt shredded beneath it.

Emotions poured out in the form of rage, and he grabbed a plastic clock from the bedside table and flung it across the room. It slammed into the wall, and the plastic face shattered. Just as he closed his eyes, a loud commotion sounded as someone kicked in the door.

Two men stormed into the bedroom.

"Get away from the female!" the tall man shouted.

From his height and the light coloring of his eyes, Kane identified him as a Chitah. He peered over his shoulder, staring at the shorter man with the comb-over who stood beside the tall tracker. Couldn't tell what Breed he was.

The Chitah lifted his fingers, holding a slip of paper between them. "Next time, take your receipt out of the bag."

The shorter man yanked Kane off the bed and cuffed his hands.

"The grocery-store manager was kind enough to rewind the footage on the security camera," the Chitah said. "People don't just leave beer sitting on the street corner, and wouldn't you know it, your victim was in the store at the same time. We managed to get his credit card information from the sale and trace it back here. You had me wasting time running around town before I realized you'd gotten into a car."

Kane winced when the cuff tightened on his wrist and pinched his skin. They could lock him up for years and it wouldn't matter; he'd already received his punishment.

"You're a sick fuck, you know that?" the man behind him growled in his ear. "Taking a dead girl back here and—Jesus, I don't even want to think about what we just walked in on!"

"Me saying goodbye," Kane murmured.

"Shut up."

The Chitah lifted a Breed badge and showed his identification. "The human police collected the body of your victim, and we confiscated all the evidence that would lead them here. It's against the law to kill a human. You're under arrest." His eyes flicked behind Kane and his nostrils flared, picking up a scent. "Was she also a human?"

"No, she's a Sensor. I did the world a favor taking out that piece of shit and leaving him for dead."

It would be the last chance Kane could look upon Caroline,

and he glanced over his shoulder. For the first time, he noticed that his socks were on her feet, and it made him slam his eyes shut. He couldn't remember her that way—lying on the bed.

No life. No light.

"Then we'll have to locate her family so they can claim the body," the Chitah grumbled. "Mick, see if she has anything on her."

Kane reached behind him with his cuffed hand and grabbed Mick by the wrist.

"Touch her and I'll end your life," he said with a visceral snarl.

The Chitah stepped forward. "Then why don't *you* tell us her name and where to send her body," he suggested in a slow and threatening voice.

"Caroline."

"Caroline what? Who does she belong to?"

Kane had never learned her last name. Did it matter? She had no one to claim her. Then the idea of her body being disposed of like unwanted trash made his stomach turn. He lifted his chin and narrowed his eyes at the Chitah.

"She's *mine*. I loved her."

He was nose to neck with the short-haired, blond tracker who glared down at him with piercing golden eyes.

"You are aware that a Chitah can scent a lie." His nostrils flared, and a muscle twitched in his face as he took in a breath of air and let it roll across his tongue. The Chitah gave Mick an unwavering stare. "He speaks the truth."

"Doesn't matter," Mick said, hooking a tight grip around Kane's arm. "We still have to haul him in for murder. Don't get all sentimental on me because of the girl. I don't give a good goddamn who he is to her; you know the laws. There was no sign of a struggle in that alley—that human was murdered in cold blood by one of ours. All that evidence left behind that we had to clean up could have led the humans into our world. I'll buy you a beer when our shift ends, and you can cry about it then."

The Chitah's mouth twisted, and he raised his hand to stop them from leaving. Something flickered in his expression, and Kane knew what it was. Chitahs revered women and would lay down their lives for one.

"Did you kill the human to protect the female?"

That could possibly get him off the hook. In the end, killing the man had kept her from an even crueler fate. Kane could have attempted to lie, but that's not how it had gone down. He killed that man out of impulse.

"No. I killed him because he was a murderer. I'm a Sensor, and his crimes are as long as the Nile."

It was almost undetectable when the Chitah shook his head. "Come with us."

Four days later, Kane was sitting on a flimsy cot in his cell. Breed jail was everything he'd heard. It was an old building with several stories, and they segregated the prisoners by their Breed. Vampires were located on the floor below, staked for their entire sentence. The wood paralyzed them. Rotting away for years without moving or eating (not that they needed to) would be enough to drive a man out of his mind.

Every six hours, a tray filled with food that came out of a can would slide beneath the bars through a rectangular gap. The meat was barely recognizable. He should have been hungry, but Kane hadn't eaten since the morning of the murder.

The guards showed up like clockwork, leaving his tray and later collecting the uneaten slop that they called food. Kane never sensed anything while touching his tray, and the guards wore gloves when making their rounds. They denied Sensors access to emotional imprints, perhaps so they couldn't uncover juicy tidbits about the guards to use as blackmail later. Guards were required to keep their distance from the cells and not engage in conversation. No doubt men had tried to bribe them with a mind-blowing emotional trip in exchange for a walk out of jail. Kane had never collected or stored useless emotions, so he had nothing to offer.

There weren't many Sensors locked away, so it was quiet. Except for the guy five cells down who liked to whistle a lot.

Kane looked down at his laceless shoes and sighed. Sleeping the first three nights had been impossible, and he doubted that tonight would be any different. Each time his eyes closed, he saw Caroline's smile, one that time would eventually try to erase. On the first night, he awoke screaming, out of control. The guard had slammed a baton against the bars as a warning. In the dream, Caroline had slipped down a black tunnel with nothing at the end. She whispered to him, but he couldn't hear the words. She should have seen a light; wasn't that what was supposed to happen? A tunnel, a light, angels or some shit?

The memory of it crippled him, and he rubbed his rough hands against his face. He'd never felt so gutted in his life.

Taking out the human was the best thing he'd ever done, but it didn't matter to the men who'd locked him up. The one thing that kept him sane was thinking about the women who wouldn't fall prey to that rabid human. They'd gotten a free pass without even knowing it.

Kane pinched his earlobe and listened to the door at the end of the hall open. Someone needed to oil the hinge because it creaked like an old house in a horror movie. He tensed, wondering if they were going to impose the death sentence. So many regrets ran through his mind, and he thought about what kind of man he might have been if he'd just given himself the chance.

Would they allow him to contact Sunny one last time? There would be no jury or trial. When they deliberated a person's fate, the facts of the case were presented to some representatives who made a collective decision. Kane faced a possible death sentence, or at the very least, a lifetime behind bars.

The footsteps grew closer, and Kane readied himself. Today was the day of his sentencing. Now he knew how Caroline must have felt, not really knowing what was coming except for the certainty that there was no escaping the inevitable.

A long shadow slithered into his cell and he swallowed hard, wringing his hands together.

"I asked if I could bring in a frying pan to cook you up some fajitas, but they wouldn't let me," a delicate voice said.

Kane's head snapped up, and his heart caught in his chest.

Standing on the other side of the bars was a lovely young brunette in a pair of jeans and a red blouse with a V-neck collar. Her hair was smooth and fell in subtle waves just past her shoulders.

Maybe in the middle of the night he had died in his sleep and this was the other side. But why would Caroline's ghost visit him in a pair of red sneakers with white laces? His body refused to move.

She swung her hip and rested a fist against it. "Well, if *that's* how you treat your visitors, I'll just go."

Caroline whirled around and disappeared.

Without a conscious thought, Kane flew up and slammed against the bars, gripping them tightly and trying to mash his face through. "No, don't go," he called out.

She slinked into view as if she'd only moved a few inches out of sight, twisting a lock of hair around her index finger.

Damn, it *was* her. Heavenly brown eyes, a glowing complexion, a cunning smirk, and she was completely eating his reaction up. The glint of the anchor between the open cut of her blouse caught his eye.

As did the luscious shape of her hips—ones that those jeans should have been flattered to hold, but instead they hung slack. Her thin T-shirt was short enough that he could see the flat of her stomach and hips. He'd never envied a pair of denims in his whole damn life until he saw them on Caroline.

"But you're dead," he said in disbelief, pressing his forehead bruisingly between the bars.

Caroline walked closer until she was within arm's reach.

"I *was* dead… for a little while. There was a strong pull somewhere else, and I was going there without a choice in the matter." Caroline sniffed as if she'd been crying, although her eyes didn't show any signs of tears. "Then your voice called out and…"

"And what?" he asked hoarsely.

She stepped closer, and it smelled as if he'd walked into a field of wildflowers during the spring when the blooms first open. A blush tinted her skin, so pale and immediate that he reached out to touch her. His finger grazed along her rosy cheek, and Kane's lips eased into a grin.

He *felt* her happiness.

Caroline's inability to transfer her emotions wasn't entirely true. Kane's gift was strong enough that he was able to pick up the slightest trace of them. It was just enough to taste her emotions, but not so much that they would overwhelm him.

Suddenly, he wanted his hands all over her skin. A deep ache knotted in his belly, turning him inside out. Before he realized what he was doing, Kane pulled at the ends of her cotton shirt until she shuffled her feet forward, only an inch away from the bars.

Her breath tickled his neck.

"And what? Finish what you were going to say," he muttered, intoxicated by her nearness, caressing the narrow curve of her waist.

"Did you mean what you said, Kane? That you loved me? I heard you say it. I felt your emotion—it formed a connection that carved a pathway back to the living world." Her eyes sparkled as she recounted the memory. "It spread out beneath my feet like brilliant diamonds, and suddenly I had a choice! Whatever was pulling me into the darkness let go, and I felt you reaching for me. It really *does* work, Kane. It wasn't your words that brought me back. It was your love. But was the love for me, or were you remembering someone else?"

He kissed her on the nose and watched her long eyelashes flutter. "It was *always* for you, angel."

This woman mattered, and he wasn't ashamed to admit it. A unique link existed between them that was effortless and natural. One that had very little to do with their abilities as Sensors and everything to do with the basic laws of attraction. His heart swelled within his chest, and Kane knew that this was the woman he was meant to be with—Caroline was the woman that his heart was anchored to.

He rubbed his nose against hers as his mouth moved lower. The tension between them became thick and magnetic. The first taste of her lips—hell, he almost groaned. They were so warm and giving, so unexpectedly familiar. His tongue stroked her bottom lip on the last kiss, and his breath trembled. Damn, she was sweet like vanilla and cherries. Kane savored every moment; tasting her in the flesh surpassed anything that they had experienced inside her head.

This was *real*.

She shyly rubbed her nose against his and stepped back.

Kane quietly chuckled as he thought about their kiss. "Why are you turning crimson? You act as if we've never—"

"We haven't," she reminded him. Her shoe squeaked against the shiny floor as she lowered her eyes and shrugged with a lift of her shoulder. "Not for real. Do you want to sit with me and talk for a little bit? I walked all the way here, and my feet are hurting in these new shoes. I didn't wear any socks, so they've been digging at my heels."

His eyes narrowed to razor-thin slivers. "You walked *all* the way here by yourself? These are dangerous streets, Caroline. I shouldn't have to tell you that." The timbre of his voice was flat and laced with disapproval. Kane pinched his left earlobe.

Imagining her out on the streets alone flared up a surge of protectiveness, and what bothered him the most was that he was locked up and unable to look out for her. He collected himself when he noticed that she was touching his left hand and using her Sensor abilities to feel his anger. Concern wrapped around her expression.

"I'm sorry," she said. "I didn't think you'd care. I promise I'll take a cab next time."

"Next time?"

She sat on her knees and Kane followed her lead, taking a seat on the floor and leaning on his left arm.

"Are you okay?" he asked as he looked over her body.

Caroline twisted her elbow, showing him a few Band-Aids. "I'll live."

He released a long sigh after hearing those two words, and it felt like he could breathe again.

"The reason I'm here, Kane, is because they gave me permission to break the news of your sentence." Her eyes lifted slowly to meet his, and when she tilted her head, a few strands of hair slipped across her face. "I talked to a bunch of men on the committee and told them everything that happened. At least, as much as you had told me. After they took you away, the Chitah stayed behind. He said that he'd sensed something was off and examined my body. That's when I came out of it. I was screaming out your name, but you weren't there."

They found each other's hands between the bars. It seemed like such a natural thing to do since all the time they had spent together, they'd been connected by touch.

"The Chitah took care of me, but I refused to let him… you know… lick me."

Kane knew. The Chitah could have healed a superficial wound with the stroke of his tongue, but if Kane had found out another man's tongue had been on Caroline, he might have gone ballistic.

"Anyhow," she continued, "they called a Relic, who showed up right away. Not much could be done at that point, and it took me a couple of days to shake off what happened. I told them everything—including how you saved me. They considered all the facts and reduced your sentence. I tried to convince them to set you free, given the fact that you saved my life, but they were firm on punishing you for the original crime. It didn't matter that the human life you took held no value and that he was a devil on the loose. You saved more lives than mine, Kane. So," she said with a proud smile, "you only have to serve a year."

A year. Damn, why did that seem like such a long time?

He flinched when her nail dug into his hand. "Don't feel that way about it. They wanted to lock you up for eighty-five years, so I think that's a pretty good deal."

"You did that… for me?"

A radiant smile brightened her face, along with the pale shimmer of lipstick that he could still taste on his tongue. "I was given special visitation rights, so I get to come up here whenever I want to. Well, as long as it's within visiting hours. Guess what else?" she asked with excitement in her voice.

He almost got up but rubbed his palm down the cotton fabric of his navy-blue pants instead. "How can you be so damn happy about coming to a prison to visit a *criminal*?"

Caroline reached between the bars and grabbed him by his collar with a tight fist.

"Because, you idiot, that *criminal* stole my heart," she said with a playful smile. "I think that entitles me to visitation rights, don't you? Before you so rudely interrupted me, they said I'm allowed to bring you food. Of course, they made a big deal about silverware."

Her thin-lipped snarl relaxed into a smile, and Kane failed miserably at concealing his grin.

"Do you want me to contact your sister and tell her where you are?"

Kane thought about it and shook his head. "No, I'd rather you didn't. I don't want her to see me in here. She doesn't know I'm a Sensor—she'd never accept this world."

He'd been distancing himself from her over the past couple of years because his aging had slowed down in his mid-twenties, and soon enough, Sunny would appear older than him.

"Maybe you shouldn't underestimate what people are willing to accept in their lives."

While she was talking, Kane reached out and lightly dabbed his finger on her cheek. She fell silent and watched him with curious eyes. He turned his wrist up and held out his finger, showing her the eyelash. No words were exchanged; she simply blew it off and they went on as normal.

Caroline leaned to her left and grabbed a sack with Coyote Burger written on the side in swirly letters. She unrolled the top and pulled out a burger wrapped in paper and a side of onion rings. They were the big patties he liked, the ones that came with extra pickles. And when his stomach growled, Caroline snickered.

"Guess that means I won't be getting any more kisses," he said, nodding at the onion rings. She might as well have brought a clove of garlic.

"Well, if you're going to be *that* way about it…"

She slid the box in front of her and lifted an onion ring to her mouth. Kane snatched it from her hand, and she laughed. They quietly sat there, watching each other as they ate a side order of onion rings. It was fucking great. Kane couldn't remember the last time he'd had such a good time, and here he was, sitting in a prison cell and sharing his lunch with a beautiful woman who was willing to wait a year for him.

He took the time to absorb everything about Caroline— the way her left eyebrow lifted up when she was giving him sass and her little habit of clearing her throat when she was nervous.

"So, I was thinking," Caroline began, "that when you get out of here, we can go shopping for an apartment together. Is that rushing?" She licked the ketchup from her thumb and peeked at him through her lashes.

"I won't have a job."

Caroline swirled her finger in the ketchup. "Don't be so pessimistic. You'll find work."

"This will be on my permanent Breed record," he reminded her, twirling his finger around to point out his surroundings. "It's not easy for an ex-con to find work unless you have family who will help."

She leaned forward and placed her face between the bars. "It'll work out, Kane. I promise. I don't need to be with a rich man, and I have a job to help pay the bills. We'll do this together."

Kane reached out and captured her wrist, gently pulling her hand through the bars. He kept his eyes locked on hers as he licked the dollop of ketchup from her index finger and then went back to eating as if nothing had happened between them. She blushed wildly and he smiled, dusting the crumbs off his hands. That's when he noticed the red scar on her head.

"Does it hurt?" he asked, his voice edged with concern.

Her eyes widened, and she reached up to touch it. "You want me to compare a cut to dying? While we're on this topic, do you mind explaining why you superglued my head together?"

That got him, and Kane completely lost it. He fell on his back, laughing harder than he had in years.

"It's not funny, Kane."

Oh God, but it was. His laughter was maniacal, and hearing her seriousness made it even worse.

Caroline slapped his leg and tried to pretend she was mad, telling him to stop. His side hurt, and he developed one of those embarrassingly silly laughs that men just don't want anyone to hear. He snorted and finally turned on his side, realizing he'd just killed any chance of keeping this woman around.

"I'm so glad I'm snort-worthy."

When the stitch in his side went away, Kane sat up, rubbing his sore face.

Caroline was smiling. "Can we do this for real?" she asked. "I want a *real* date."

A hopeful look flashed in her eyes as she nervously tore at the edge of the wrapper. He felt the connection just as surely as she did—as if they were old lovers rediscovering one another after meeting up in a new life. They'd gotten to know each other on such a personal level, and yet everything felt like the first time.

This was real.

"Okay," he agreed, scooting toward the bars. "As long as

you don't mention to our kids where we had our first date. Deal?"

Her apple cheeks blossomed, and she lifted her lovely eyes. They were earthy and so full of life and kindness. She gave him a short nod, and he nodded back.

"What's your full name?"

"Caroline Marie Potter."

He almost spit out the onion ring he had just eaten. "Your last name is Potter?"

Her lips shrank into thin lines. "Yeah."

"And you like to go by *Carrie*?"

"Don't say it," she warned, waving a finger. "I didn't have any problems until those books came out. My turn." She unwrapped another burger and pulled out a pickle, tossing it into her mouth. "Where were you born?"

"California. Why would you want to waste a year of your life visiting a murderer?"

"One who saved my life? Next question."

He pulled the edge of the wrapper nearer to the bars and fed her a pickle. She happily took it and shifted her legs to sit Indian style.

"Favorite food?" she asked.

"Fish tacos."

Her nose wrinkled. "Ew."

Kane arched a brow. "Since when did you become the culinary snob?"

"Since you started putting a sea animal into a tortilla."

"Fish," he corrected.

She waved a hand. "Whatever. So tell me, do you have a nickname? You seem to enjoy teasing me about mine."

Kane clamped his mouth shut and scratched the side of his neck.

Her eyes brightened. "This should be good. Tell me."

Shit. He couldn't lie to this woman. He looked her straight in the eye, his expression serious. "Snoopy."

His sister had given him the nickname, and it was something that only she called him. He waited for Caroline to laugh and make fun of it, but the muscles relaxed in her face and she chewed slowly—thoughtfully.

"I like that you're honest with me, Kane. I'm sure there's a story behind it that you'll tell me someday."

"Do you mind that I call you Caroline? I can stop if it bothers you." He hadn't thought about it, but maybe there was a reason why she went by the shorter version.

Soft hair shook in front of her face. "No. I don't mind at all. Favorite color?"

Easy, he thought. When he spoke, his voice was thick like honey. "Red."

Caroline twisted her mouth to the side and leaned forward with a doubtful look. "I thought it was blue?"

He looked at her blouse, gaze full of admiration. "Today it's red."

"Why?" she asked. A tiny line pinched between her brows.

Kane wedged his face between the bars. He knew his eyes were doing that seduction thing again by the way she averted her gaze. The charm on her neck glittered in the light and constricted his heart.

"Because of this," he said, touching the soft fabric of her blouse. "You wore this for *me*. Ask me what my favorite color is ten years from now and it's going to be red."

"Ten years?" she asked in disbelief.

Kane lifted her chin with the crook of his finger. He smoothed the hair away from her face, gently touching the scar that she would carry for years to come. She closed her eyes for a moment and he felt her, and she was glowing with hope. When he had her full attention, his hand slid down her arm until his fingertips curled around her wrist. With that single touch, he felt her pulse, her warmth, her life, and he wanted to prove his sincerity to this woman who looked at him with such adoration and yet wasn't afraid to put him in his place.

Kane hadn't saved her that night—she'd saved him.

"My turn, angel. How many kids do you want?" he asked. "Because when I get out of here, you and me are making lots of babies."

Printed in Great Britain
by Amazon

82820448R00089